Until She Says Yes

Tricia Linden

Kingsburg Press
San Francisco, California

Kingsburg Press
P.O. Box 475146
San Francisco, California, 94147
www.KingsburgPress.com

Until She Says Yes is a work of fiction. Names, characters, places, and incidents are a product of the author's imagination. Locales and public names are sometimes used for atmospheric purposes. Any resemblance to actual people, living or dead, or to businesses, companies, events, institutions, or locales is completely coincidental.

Editor: Deborah Fallon
Cover Design: RLSather @ SelfPubBookCovers.com

ISBN- 13:978-1-946177-11-7
ISBN- 10: 1-946177-11-3
eBook ISBN: 978-1-946177-12-4

Other Books of Timeless Romance by Tricia Linden

Jules Vanderzeit novels

set in the Gilded Age of New York

Until We Meet Again

Until Their Hearts Desire

Until You Love Me

.

.

.

The MacNicol Clan Through Time

A Time To Begin – Book 1

A Time To Return – Book 2

A Time To Belong – Book 3

A Time To Forgive – Book 4

.

.

.

Dreaming In Moonlight

.

Dedication
Cynthia B, my dear friend
for so many years. Thanks

CHAPTER 1

New York City, December 1894

Kingsley Goddard felt a trickle of trepidation drip down his back. This should be a moment of joyful anticipation, but when dealing with the Vanderbilts one could never be sure. The seemingly simple act of asking a woman to be your wife was daunting enough, but when the woman of one's desire was the daughter of Alva Vanderbilt, daunting didn't begin to describe his concerns.

Consuelo had informed him that her father, William Vanderbilt, was away, cruising along the Atlantic coast on his yacht. That left her mother, Alva Vanderbilt, to contend with. The self-proclaimed matron of society was known for being unpredictable, pompous and bossy. Kingsley had already been kept waiting in the reception foyer for longer than usual while the Vanderbilts' butler announced his arrival. Considering he had been calling on Consuelo Vanderbilt for the past few months, his visit should not seem unexpected. Consuelo had assured him she would be at home with her mother this afternoon, and he had arrived promptly at two o'clock, the earliest proper time for receiving visitors.

When he was finally shown to the drawing room, he was received by Consuelo and her mother sitting side by side on a dark burgundy settee. Notably absent was the presence of a tea cart or other form of refreshment. It seemed the only thing Mrs. Vanderbilt was prepared to

1

offer him as a guest in her house was a stern look of disapproval. It didn't bode well for what he had in mind.

"Mrs. Vanderbilt, Miss Vanderbilt, good afternoon to you both." Kingsley gave the ladies a slight bow before taking his seat across from them.

Mrs. Vanderbilt addressed him formally, with a raised chin. "Mr. Goddard, Consuelo tells me you have something important you want to discuss. It that correct?"

It seemed Mrs. Vanderbilt was in a hurry to get right to the point of his visit. Another trickle of trepidation dripped down his back. Might as well get on with this. "As I am sure you know, Mrs. Vanderbilt, I have been calling on your daughter for some time now, and I believe we have developed a very close affection for one another." Kingsley glanced at Consuelo and she gave him a nervous half smile, but her eyes seemed sad. This wasn't looking good.

"Yes, I am aware. Not that I necessarily approve." Mrs. Vanderbilt's curt reply set Kingsley's pulse racing. While he knew Consuelo's mother had a tendency to bluntly speak her mind, he hadn't expected such a discourteous response.

With pleading eyes, it seemed Consuelo wished him to continue. Setting aside his displeasure with Mrs. Vanderbilt, Kingsley took a deep breath and stated his proposal. "Surely, you understand I wish to marry your daughter. And she has expressed her agreement to such a union. I've come to ask for her hand in marriage."

"I care not what my daughter may or may not have expressed. The answer is no. That is simply not possible," Mrs. Vanderbilt stated firmly.

"But, Mother, I love him," Consuelo cried as she scooted away from her mother.

"I will lock you in your room before I will allow you to marry this man. You are meant for royalty—a duke or a prince—not the son of a banker. He's nothing more than an engineer, for Christ's sake."

Kingsley had never felt so mortified in all his life. Mrs. Vanderbilt was known for being pugnacious and difficult, but never had he expected she would claim he wasn't good enough for her daughter. To think this woman might have been his mother-in-law was enough to turn his stomach.

"I don't want a duke or a prince. I want Kingsley." Consuelo continued to plead, but Kingsley could see the cause was lost.

Mrs. Vanderbilt glared harshly at her daughter. "I don't care what you want."

"Mother, you can't mean that!" Consuelo seemed on the verge of tears.

"Stop it, Consuelo. I won't have it." Mrs. Vanderbilt reached out and firmly gripped her daughter's hand, causing Consuelo to wince.

Kingsley feared Mrs. Vanderbilt was two heartbeats away from slapping her daughter right there in front of him. For Consuelo's sake, he stood to make his departure. "Please, excuse me. It seems I have been mistaken in my perception. It was not my intent to cause such discord." Nor did he wish to stay where he wasn't welcomed.

As much as he cared for her, at this point, even if Consuelo's mother were to give her consent, he refused to have Alva Vanderbilt as his mother-in-law. "Good day to you, Consuelo. I wish you all the best."

"But Kingsley . . ." Consuelo looked as if she were about to rise and join him, but her mother clutched her wrist and held her down.

"I'm sorry, Consuelo, really I am." Before the scene could get any uglier than it already was, Kingsley turned on his heel and exited the room. When the butler met him in the entrance foyer with his coat and hat, Kingsley angrily grabbed them from the servant and hurried out the door, vowing he would never again step foot inside another Vanderbilt residence as long as he lived.

~*~

Village of Ferentino, Italy, January 1895

"Shut up, Pappa. Just shut up. Good lord, must you always yell at everyone? Can't you just let us be?" Anna Maria Lucci had never spoken such harsh words to her father before, but after spending a year away in London, she was no longer willing to stand by and meekly accept his

3

wrath. When he raised his hand to strike her, she lifted her chin in defiance. *Let him slap me, it can be no worse than his words.* To her surprise, he held back, and lowered his hand.

Like so many times before, Anna's father had spent the morning yelling at anyone who crossed his path, including her mother, her sisters, and even her youngest brother, Marco. Only this time, Anna Maria could no longer take it. The breaking point came when her younger sisters ran to her bedroom to hide from their father as he shouted at Marco, while their mother stood by and did nothing. No one, it seemed, was willing to stand up to her father, except her.

"It seems your time in London has taught you disrespect," her father barked, clenching his fists at his side. "I knew it was a bad idea to let you go with Carlo, and I was right. But no, your mother insisted time away would be good for you. Send our eldest daughter off to see the world, she said. The education would be good for you. Now look at the woman you've become. I'm ashamed." He was no longer shouting, but his words were just as harsh.

"You're ashamed! I'm ashamed. Marco is too young to defend himself, but I'm not." She would rather risk her father's wrath than meekly stand by and do nothing.

"Mark my words, Anna Maria, someday you will regret your actions. Until you learn to behave as a proper lady should, you'll never find a man who will take you as a wife. No man wants a shrew for a wife." Antonio Lucci turned his back on his daughter and walked away.

That he was no longer yelling at her siblings was her only solace. When she looked to her mother for comfort and support, all she saw was silent condemnation.

Feeling more hurt than she cared to admit, Anna Maria stomped out the front door of her family home and into the street. Regret and pain pounded hard in her chest. He was wrong. Her time away in London hadn't made her disrespectful, nor improper. Strong-minded, yes, and perhaps a little too independent, but not improper. Her Pappa, however, was as strict and hardhearted as ever.

4

Anna hurried across the street, hoping to take refuge at her aunt's house until her father's anger subsided. Zia Camilla lived only a few blocks away and Anna had often sought her company when tensions at home became unbearable. The streets were still wet from the early morning rain, causing Anna to trip on the slippery, uneven cobblestones paving the street. Unable to regain her footing, she lost her balance and fell head first into the path of a fast approaching rider. Screaming, she threw up her hands in front of her face, certain the horse and rider would run her down.

For a brief moment, it felt as though she were flying, twirling over the cobblestones, and then an instant later, she felt strong hands pull her to safety.

When her fear subsided and her breathing returned to normal, Anna Maria miraculously found herself sitting on a wrought iron bench on the far side of the road. Standing next to her was an older man she had not seen before.

"Are you all right, my dear?" The man, obviously of wealth and taste, spoke English with a refined American accent and wore an expensive, dark grey suit.

Badly shaken, but still in one piece, Anna nodded tentatively. "I believe so, Signore, with thanks to you," she replied, also speaking in English.

"That was a close one. I almost thought I had lost you. Timing is everything, you know." He reached out a hand and helped her to stand. "Are you able to walk?"

"I think so." Accepting his assistance, Anna rose to her feet and looked about. Strangely, she was much farther from her house than she would have guessed.

"You know, in this world, sometimes one misstep is all it takes. Now then, I believe you may have been headed to your aunt's house before you took that nasty fall. Do you mind if I accompany you and we can talk?"

Anna pulled back from the man with apprehension. "How do you know this?"

5

"Ah, there is much I know about you, Signorina Lucci, and much we need to discuss." Holding out his arm for her to take, he added, "Shall we?"

She took a step back. "I do not know you, Signore. This would not be proper." *Americans!* They were known for being pushy, especially the rich ones, which judging by the man's clothes and manner of speech, would apply to him.

"Allow me to introduce myself, I am Jules Vanderzeit." He reached into the front pocket of his coat, pulled out a card, and handed it to her.

Jules Vanderzeit

Maestro

"You are a conductor of music?" Anna smiled optimistically.

"While I am a great lover of music, I prefer to conduct time, and fate, and all manner of destiny."

"Conduct time?" Though it wasn't her native language, Anna had spent the last year studying English while in London with her younger brother Carlo, and believed she was fluent in the language. But Signore Vanderzeit's words were lost on her. She had never heard anyone use such a phrase as *conduct time*.

"Perhaps, if you are not up for walking, we can rest a while in the café down the street. Come, I will buy you a drink while we discuss your future."

"My future, Signore? I have only just met you." Her earlier concerns about speaking with this strange man returned.

"Yes, but I've had my eye on you for quite some time. If you're interested, there's an opportunity for you to live and work in New York. But, of course, only if you are willing to take such a chance."

Live in New York? While the opportunity to travel to New York held great appeal, it was not something she had ever considered. Many called America the land of opportunity, but to her it seemed a distant, foreign country on the far side of an ocean. Such a momentous decision was not something to be taken lightly, and certainly not based on a brief conversation with a man she had just met in the street. True, he had

6

rescued her from harm, but that didn't mean she could trust him, much less, believe what he was saying.

Still, she was interested. Perhaps it wouldn't hurt to hear what he had to say, as long as she proceeded with caution. "I cannot say if I will accept your offer, but I am willing to hear what you have to say."

"Excellent. That's all I ask, Miss Lucci. Fate can handle the rest." Signore Vanderzeit escorted her to the nearby café and ordered them each a coffee with cream. Once they were settled with their drinks, he began to explain. "I understand you have recently returned from studying abroad in London, am I right?"

"How do you know this?" While she had not actually attended the university with her brother—that was more than her father would allow—she had been his constant study partner. Besides learning English, she had studied several other subjects using the books her brother brought home from his college classes.

"You speak English quite well; your Aunt Camilla is very proud of you. She believes you will go on to do great things, and I believe she may be right, if you are willing to accept my offer."

"You know my aunt? Why didn't you say so earlier?" Anna Maria felt a wave of relief wash through her. If her beloved Zia Camilla was friends with this man, surely he could be trusted.

"I don't believe I had an opportunity. Now, if I may proceed, there's a family traveling through Italy with young children who are in need of a governess. At the end of summer, they plan to return to New York, and will want to take their new Italian governess with them. I would like to place you in this position. Before you decide, I hasten to add, I did save your life back there when you were in danger of being run over."

While Anna Maria was grateful for the assistance he had provided, she believed Signore Vanderzeit might be overstating his role in her fall. Rescued her from harm, certainly, but to say he saved her life seemed a bit excessive. However, that was not nearly important as the opportunity he offered. "Should I not first meet this family? I'm sure they will want some assurance I am capable for the job."

"They are currently staying in Rome. Mrs. Dover is so taken with the culture of Italy, she is quite insistent her children should learn to speak Italian from a *proper* Italian governess. You are a proper Italian, are you not, Signorina Lucci?"

"You would not ask such a thing, if you know Zia Camilla, as you say." While her father had just accused her of being improper, and disrespectful, Anna did not share his assessment. Pappa was a well-established merchant in their village with the financial resources to send his eldest son for a year to a university in London. Zia Camilla, Pappa's sister, lived in a fine house near the center of town. Certainly, there could be no doubt she was a proper young lady from a proper and respected Italian family.

"While I respect your aunt, *you* are the important one here. Next week, Mrs. Dover and her five children will travel on to Pompeii. You must meet with them tomorrow, if you wish to pursue this path. I will make the necessary arrangements."

Five children! Anna had not thought there would be so many. She needed to speak with her own family, of course, but if her aunt was willing to vouch for Signore Vanderzeit, Anna felt certain her father would give his necessary approval. At least she hoped he would.

As if reading her thoughts, Signore Vanderzeit added, "Go visit your aunt to get her opinion, if you think it will help."

"I was on my way to see her when you came to my aid. If she confirms what you say, and agrees this is a good situation, Signore Vanderzeit, then yes, I will consider your proposal."

"Splendid. I'll be at your aunt's house tomorrow morning to take you to Rome."

How very presumptuous of him. "But I haven't accepted, yet."

"I've no doubt you will. We'll travel by train. I'm sure your aunt will want to accompany us as your chaperone. Please be prepared to stay with the family if they agree take you on, which I am certain they will."

His confidence in her was both flattering and reassuring. "How would I repay you?" she asked, thinking mainly about the cost of the train tickets.

8

"You need not worry about that now. When the time is right, I am sure you will do the right thing. What's important now is to set this path in motion."

"I am grateful, Signore. If what you say is true, I look forward to seeing you tomorrow."

Anna Maria bid farewell to Mr. Vanderzeit, and hurried off to her aunt's house, anxious to tell her all that had happened with both her father and Mr. Vanderzeit. Though she was intrigued by his offer, there was still the possibility she might refuse. First, she would need the approval of her father, and before that happened, she would have to apologize for her outburst, which wasn't a pleasant thought. As she entered through her aunt's kitchen door, Anna was somewhat dismayed to see her mother was also there, waiting for her.

"Anna Maria, my little bambino, what have you done?" Zia Camilla asked, rising from her chair at the kitchen table to greet her.

"More importantly, where did you go?" Mamma asked, but remained seated.

Anna's gaze darted between her mother and Zia Camilla. Both wore grave expressions of concern. Were they really that worried over her slight delay? Her brief conversation with Signore Vanderzeit couldn't have lasted more than fifteen or twenty minutes.

"When I . . . when I ran out of the house, I planned to come here, but I fell in the street and a kind man came to my assistance. Signore Jules Vanderzeit. He said he knows you," Anna said, accepting a hug and kiss from her aunt.

Surprisingly, there was no similar greeting from her mother.

"You don't look hurt," Mamma said curtly.

Anna looked down at her skirt, expecting to see signs of her tumble in the street such as dirt stains or a tear in the fabric, but there was nothing. Even the palms of her hands appeared uninjured. It was a marvel she had survived unscathed.

Before she could answer to defend herself, Mamma continued. "What you said to your father is unforgivable. I'm sorry to say, he does not want you back in the house."

9

Shocked, Anna clung to her aunt. "You can't be serious?" Certainly, once his temper had cooled, he would let her return home. If not today, surely by tomorrow.

"Anna Maria, do you think I would jest about something so serious? This is not the first time you have evoked his anger. None of this would have even happened if you had agreed to marry Signore Tarantino."

How could Mamma say such a thing? She had believed her mother supported her refusal to marry Giulio Tarantino. Besides being twelve years older than Anna, he was the village butcher, and often smelled of blood and rotten meat. One of the reasons her father had agreed to send her off to London with her brother had been to remove the sting of her being unmarried from the view of their neighbors.

"I'm sure if we give him a chance to cool off, he'll change his mind," Anna said, hoping it was true.

Mamma shook her head. "Not this time. I'm afraid you've gone too far."

"But Mamma, surely you understand why I did it. He was yelling at Marco." She always had a soft spot for her youngest brother. Besides being the baby of the family with four older sisters to contend with, as the long awaited second son, their father placed nearly unobtainable expectations upon him. As a result, Anna felt a need to defend Marco much like a mother hen with her chicks. "I'll apologize to Pappa, if it means that much to him."

"You should apologize, but I doubt it will make much difference."

Anna felt as if she had been struck. "But Mamma!"

"I've spoken to your aunt. Camilla agrees to let you stay here until something else can be arranged." Mamma glanced at Camilla, who nodded in approval.

Anna Maria instantly thought of Signore Vanderzeit's offer. It couldn't have come at a more opportune time. Lifting her chin, she stated, "You needn't worry, Mamma. While I appreciate Zia Camilla's generous hospitality, it turns out I've been offered a job as a governess for an American family traveling in Italy." Anna turned to her aunt and added, "It was from Signore Vanderzeit. He assured me you would approve."

"Oh my. I would never refuse Signore Vanderzeit. I owe him so much. If not for him, I never would have met my husband."

"I thought you met Giancarlo through his mother. How could that have involved this Signore Vanderzeit?" Anna's mother asked.

"Oh, you know, it was all in the past, a good long time ago, but I can assure you, if he says he needs your services, I suggest you go. It's never good to refuse the Maestro." Zia Camilla gave a reassuring pat atop Anna's hand.

"He's a Maestro?" Mamma asked, sounding impressed.

"Yes, here's his card." Anna pulled the card from her pocket and handed it to her mother. There was no need to mention what he had said about conducting time, since it made no sense anyway.

"He has recommended you to serve as a governess?" Mamma examined the card with a look of disbelief.

Disappointed by her mother's lack of faith, Anna took a seat at the table across from her, more determined than ever to take the position and move to America. "Apparently, the family is anxious for me to start right away. I need to leave tomorrow." To her aunt, she added, "Is it all right if I stay the night? I'll just need to return to the house to gather my things."

"And apologize to your father," her mother stated firmly.

"Yes, Mamma, and apologize to Pappa." It was probably best not to leave with unnecessary anger hanging between them, if it could be avoided.

While she dearly loved her parents, she resented her father's anger. Far too often, Antonio Lucci's temper was directed at his wife and children. Her time spent in London studying with Carlo, though often being lonely and demanding, had given her freedom from her father's tirades. Serving as her elder brother's housekeeper and companion while he attended university hadn't always been easy—she'd been alone in a foreign city, learning a foreign language, with only her brother to rely on—but the sense of independence and self-reliance she had gained from the experience was more than worth the effort. Her greatest regret had been the day Carlo informed her they had to return to their father's home in Ferentino, Italy. Now she had an opportunity to travel to America, and there was no one to stop her.

CHAPTER 2

New York City, June 1, 1895

Anna Maria glanced up at the clock on the schoolroom wall and saw her time with the children was almost over. They had time for one more song: *Bella Farfallina*, Beautiful Butterfly, sung in Italian. Soon after Anna began working with the children, she had asked that they only speak Italian during her lessons with them to quicken their exposure to the language. For the youngest ones, it was not always easy, and they often reverted to English when they had something important they wanted to share, but they were so much better now than when she had first met them.

Bouncing on her toes and swaying to the music, Anna Maria waved her hands through the air, tapping out the beats of the music as the children's voices filled the room. It was such a joy to be their governess. Considering she needed to work for her living—which Anna Maria did—this was the best possible job she could hope for.

Right on time, as usual, the children's nursemaid stepped into the classroom to take them to lunch. The children would be under the nursemaid's supervision until the next governess began her classes. While they were in Italy, Anna had been the only governess for the children, teaching them Italian as well as several other subjects, and touring with them through the cities they visited. Since moving with the family to New York, she had become one of three women providing care and lessons to Mrs. Dover's children, and had more time on her hands

13

than ever before. Their regular nursemaid was responsible for their meals, clothes, or daily routines, and the afternoon governess taught them French and mathematics. Anna's Italian and music lessons with the five children were for two hours a day, six days a week. She also spent an hour or two each day preparing the lessons and checking the children's progress on their daily worksheets. Other than that, her time was her own and she spent much of it reading books borrowed from the Dovers' extensive library. The routine had helped improve her knowledge of English as the Dovers had very few books in other languages.

She was about to return to the quite solitude of the library to find something new to read when Mrs. Dover's personal maid informed her she was needed in the drawing room. When she entered the room, a woman she had not seen before was with her employer.

"Anna Maria, I'm glad you could join us. Perfect timing. How were the children this morning?" Mrs. Dover greeted her.

"Perfect, as always. They've learned a new song, Beautiful Butterfly, and are doing quite well." Mrs. Dover didn't usually call her in to ask about the children, and it made Anna wonder why she was doing so now.

"Anna Maria, this is Mrs. George Goddard. She's interested in obtaining the services of an Italian governess," Mrs. Dover said as Anna stood before her. To her guest, she added, "Her name is Anna Maria Lucci. I'm sure you'll be quite happy with her."

The abrupt introduction left Anna Maria speechless. Nothing had alerted her to the idea that Mrs. Dover intended to let her go. Everything seemed to be going so well with the children. She loved living with the Dovers in their big house on Fifth Avenue, and teaching the children songs in Italian, even if it did mean she had to share a room with the French governess.

"Are you displeased with my services?" Anna asked Mrs. Dover.

Mrs. Dover waved a bejeweled hand through the air. "Not at all. Quite the contrary. You've done a splendid job; we simply no longer need you." Indicating the woman sitting next to her, Mrs. Dover

14

continued, "My dear friend, Mrs. Goddard, is in need of a governess who can speak Italian, and of course I've recommended you. You should be honored."

"She's younger than I expected," Mrs. Goddard commented.

"I can assure you, she's been quite good with the children," Mrs. Dover said in Anna's defense.

"Yes, but mine are older." Mrs. Goddard seemed less than impressed by Mrs. Dover's words of praise, and even less considerate of the fact that Anna was standing in the room.

"Vivien and Helen will love her," Mrs. Dover replied.

"It's Howard I'm thinking of. He's at a very impressionable age." From the way Mrs. Goddard spoke, she made it sound as if Anna planned to tempt the boy with her wicked ways.

"My goodness, you don't think . . . ?" Placing her hand over her heart, Mrs. Dover had the good grace to look offended, although Anna suspected it was more about her good judgment and less about Anna's reputation.

What exactly did Mrs. Goddard think she would do to her young Howard? Run off with the boy? Good Lord, Anna was a Roman Catholic. Just because she didn't attend the same church as these women didn't mean her religious morals were any less strict. Based on their less than Christian attitudes, she suspected she was far stricter in her morals than either of them.

And why did these women think it was acceptable to talk about her as if she weren't in the room? Until now, she hadn't thought of Mrs. Dover as rude, but the current situation had Anna questioning her judgment.

"Miranda, please, I would never think such a thing, but surely you can understand my concern. She can't be more than a few years older than my Howard, and he'll be home this summer from his first year at university. Harvard, of course, like my other two boys."

"I believe she just turned twenty-two. Isn't that right, Anna Maria?" Mrs. Dover asked.

Anna simply nodded, feeling too dumbfounded to actually address either of the women, including her soon-to-be former employer.

Turning back to her guest, Mrs. Dover continued, "And Howard is what? Barely eighteen? Surely, she's old enough to be of no interest to such a young lad. I'm sure you have nothing to worry about. As for me, should we ever return to Italy, I feel the children will have no problems with the language. Even little Cindi can speak Italian quite well. However, this winter we plan to visit Spain. I've always wanted to see Barcelona. Since you're looking for a new governess to teach your children Italian, I want you to have *Signorina* Lucci. My friends deserve only the best." Mrs. Dover looked smugly happy with herself, as if she were gifting away one of her prized paintings.

Which also meant Mrs. Dover didn't care one bit about Anna, or her feelings. She'd been a fool to become so attached to the family, especially the children. And now she had to leave, because Mrs. Dover said so, and because her employer's friend, Mrs. Goddard, needed a new governess.

It had never occurred to Anna that Mrs. Dover would simply hand her off to another family without discussing the matter with her first. What if she didn't want to work for Mrs. Goddard? Had anyone thought of that? Of course, in all honesty, she had very few options, but still, a little consideration regarding her feelings in the matter would be nice.

Back home in Italy, when she had told her father about becoming a governess for Mrs. Dover and her family, his first reaction had been to say, "You'll never make it. I doubt you'll last six months. Rich folks won't tolerate having a disrespectful woman as a governess for their precious children." And now, here she was being rejected from her first job.

But she hadn't been disrespectful to the Dovers. She had done her best to be prim and proper. So regardless how badly Mrs. Dover's actions bruised her pride, she was determined to make this work. Otherwise, she risked being forced to return home, and admitting her father had been right.

Swallowing her initial reaction of pride, she quickly decided she would take the job Mrs. Goddard offered, no matter how odious she found the woman. This wasn't about what she wanted. It was about getting the next job and staying independent of her father's support.

"If she's as good as you say, then I accept," Mrs. Goddard said with resignation. "She's certainly better than nothing, and I rather have my heart set on getting an Italian governess for the children. Especially since the last governess we had wasn't very nice to Jayson. She was from Germany, you know. Of course, British governesses are the best, but they're so hard to come by and they rarely speak foreign languages. When can she be available?"

"As soon as you wish. Her lessons are done for the day," Mrs. Dover said, looking quite happy and cheerful that she was able to satisfy her friend. She gave Anna a sideways glance. "Isn't that correct, Anna Maria?"

"Well, yes, Mrs. Dover, but what about the children? Don't they matter?" Surely, this abrupt upheaval couldn't be good for the children.

"Of course, they matter," Mrs. Dover stated. "Why do you think I waited until your lesson was over?"

"Since we're planning to return to Riverwood tomorrow, I'm hoping to have this new governess settled before we leave New York. You're a lifesaver, Miranda." Mrs. Goddard seemed no more concerned about the Dover children's feelings than their mother.

"Marvelous. I am so happy this works for you. Do you wish to take Anna Maria with you now, or should we send her over to your house later today?" Mrs. Dover continued to address her guest without a glance at Anna.

"By all means, send her over later. I'm meeting Bernice Dorvall at the Park View after I leave here and I don't wish to make her wait. I'll send word to my housekeeper to expect her arrival," Mrs. Goddard answered promptly.

"Will I be allowed to say goodbye to the children?" Anna asked. This seemed unreasonably short notice for her to take up a position elsewhere.

17

"Well, yes, of course, you should say goodbye to the children. We don't want them to think you ran off without saying goodbye. That wouldn't be very nice of you, now would it," said Mrs. Dover.

Nice! Who was Mrs. Dover to be thinking about what was nice when she was basically handing Anna off to one of her friends as if she were no more important than some school books she no longer needed.

Turning back to her friend, Mrs. Dover added, "I'll have her sent over before nightfall. It's unseemly to have the servants traveling alone after dark."

"It's wonderful how you always have their best interests at heart." Mrs. Goddard smiled sweetly at Mrs. Dover while both women continued to ignore Anna.

Is that what she calls this? Having my best interests at heart? If that were the case, Mrs. Dover should have consulted her first before placing her in such an awkward position as to stand before these two women while her future was decided.

A moment later, she was dismissed from the room and advised to prepare for her transfer to her new position. When she told the nursemaid she was leaving, Aliza was quick to point out how lucky she was.

"Usually, they just tell you they no longer need your services and you're out on your ear with only a reference, if you're lucky. Mrs. Dover must think awfully highly of you to have taken the effort to find you a new home before sending you on your way."

Hearing it like that, Anna supposed she should be grateful, but still, she couldn't completely overlook how callously the exchange had taken place. While it seemed she had no right to expect better, she did. Being handed off from one wealthy matron to another wasn't what she had anticipated when she came to America, but like it or not, obviously this was how things were done here.

As she packed her few possessions into her leather satchel, Anna mentally reprimanded herself. When she took the position of governess with the Dover family, she had believed she would stay with the family until the children were grown. Such an idea now seemed overly optimistic and obviously unrealistic. No doubt, her irrational reaction to her father's ire, and her previous taste of freedom in the far-flung city of London, had played a significant role in her impulsive decision to come to America with the Dovers. At the time, exchanging the freedom she had known in London for the adventure of life in New York had seemed like a bright idea. After Anna Maria had quarreled with her father, and had nearly gotten herself killed when she ran headlong into the street, Mr. Vanderzeit's offer of a job in New York had seemed as if fate itself had intervened to change her life. Now she was second-guessing her choices.

But there was no advantage to looking back for too long since it wasn't the direction she wanted to travel. Onward and upward, or at least forward, was where she needed to focus, and hope for the best with this new family, the Goddards.

She barely had time to pack her belongings before she was given a few moments with the children to say her goodbyes.

"Not another one," Henry grumbled, folding his arms over his chest with a pout. "Mama never lets them stay." At twelve years old, he was the eldest of the five Dover children and had undoubtedly seen more governesses come and go than his younger siblings.

"Must you leave so soon?" little Martha whined, tugging at her skirt.

"We've only just begun to learn the Butterfly song." Cindi added, holding onto her older sister's hand.

"It is not up to me, little ones. It's for your mother to decide, and she has asked me to help Mrs. Goddard teach her children to learn Italian, as you have all done so well." Anna Maria hated being the bearer of bad news, but it seemed Mrs. Dover had left the dirty work with her. For this moment of farewell, the children were speaking English, and she did nothing to correct them otherwise. Such strong emotions should be expressed in their native language without being filtered through the process of translation.

"But we like you," Peter stated, stomping his foot. "We rarely like our governesses."

"The ones we like always seem to leave," Willy, the middle child, said. "Only the truly bad ones stay."

"This isn't easy for me either, children. I shall miss you all, but perhaps I shall see you again." Though she highly doubted her words, Anna Maria offered what little solace she could to the children she had grown to love during her stay with them.

"That's what they all say, but it never happens." Peter wiped his nose with the back of his hand and sniffed.

Anna Maria pulled a plain, cotton handkerchief from her pocket and handed it to Peter. "Please, use this. And you can keep it."

"I shall miss you, *Signorina* Lucci." Henry rushed to give her a hug and just as quickly, fled from the room.

Anna hugged and kissed each of the other children before retreating down the servant's stairs and out the back door. Within minutes, she was whisked off to a new, larger mansion several blocks up Fifth Avenue to begin her service to Mrs. Goddard and her family.

~*~

Kingsley stood in his father's library and scanned the shelves, certain he would eventually find what he was looking for. He could see the book clearly in his mind, and remembered referring to it while he was in engineering school. He just needed to find it among the several hundred books his father had collected over the years. Some wealthy men collected art, while others collected stables full of horses and fine coaches. George Goddard collected books; old, new and everything in between. When Kingsley had shown an interest in architecture and engineering, his father had bought every book he could find on the subjects. It was Father's way of showing his support, supplying a readily available library of reference books, even though it was no secret he hoped one of his sons would one day follow in his footsteps and take on the family's banking business. Kingsley, however, was fascinated with city planning and municipal water management and he had already made quite a name for himself as an innovator in the rapidly expanding field.

The smell and heft of books were like old familiar friends to Kingsley. It was always a pleasure to see them again, and spend time with them. This library, like the one his father maintained at their summer home on the Hudson River, always seemed a rather somber place, almost reverent in its honored role as caretaker of written knowledge. In these books were stored the thoughts and ideas of learned men who had gone before him. Kingsley breathed deeply with an almost lustful desire to absorb the words stored in these books, many written by men he admired. Unfortunately, that wasn't possible. Like all mere mortals, he had to actually read the books to unlock their secrets.

Having scanned everything at eye level and below, Kingsley was about to climb up the library ladder to begin searching the upper shelves when his father walked into the room.

"Looking for something in particular?" Father asked.

"I distinctly remember seeing a book on Roman architecture while I was studying at university and was hoping I could find it."

"You're in the right section. Can you be more specific?"

"Ancient Roman architecture, and public baths. The one I'm looking for is in Italian."

"Then it's probably up there on the second shelf." Father pointed to an area above Kingsley's head.

Using the ladder to reach the upper shelf, Kingsley quickly found what he was looking for.

"Foreign language books are always shelved near the top or bottom. I like to keep the English tomes in the middle. Easier for me to find what I want," Father said as Kingsley stepped down from the ladder.

Although Kingsley and his siblings were taught a number of foreign languages, including French, Spanish, and Italian, his father read very little that wasn't in English. It wasn't for lack of knowledge. George Goddard had been educated at the finest schools and could speak the same languages his children had been taught, he simply didn't enjoy the effort it took to read them.

Like his father before him, Kingsley's father had made his considerable fortune in banking, and shrewd investments in transportation. More than once, Kingsley had heard his father say, "We live in a mobile society. Take the people where they want to go and they will pay you for it." And yet, Kingsley was interested in neither banking nor transportation, unless it involved the transportation of water through pipes.

Kingsley flipped open the book and began scanning the pages. "Humm, it seems I may need to brush up on my Italian. I haven't used it for a couple of years. I've gotten rusty."

"How convenient. Your mother recently hired a new Italian governess for the children," Father said, referring to Kingsley's younger brothers and sisters. "Maybe she can give you some lessons. They're out at Riverwood for the summer and I know your mother would appreciate a visit from you."

"If I can find the time. I'm working with Max Branson on the engineering for a public bathing facility he's been commissioned to build for the Newport resort. I thought it might be helpful to refer to some original examples." Kingsley lifted the book in his hand as he spoke.

"Go right to the source. Sounds like a good idea." There was a sense of pride in Father's smile.

With his eyes still scanning the pages of the book he held in his hands, Kingsley mused, "Maybe I should meet Mother's new governess." He could probably muddle through on his own, but his father's comment about going to the source struck a chord. Looking up, he added, "You say she's from Italy?"

"Fresh off the boat, relatively speaking."

"Does she speak English well?"

"Better than you would expect. She spent a year in London. Came highly recommended by Miranda Dover. They employed her while they were vacationing in Italy last winter. They visited Rome and Pompeii as I recall."

"I know the Dovers. They take their children someplace warm every winter." Kingsley liked the idea of visiting Rome and Pompeii himself someday, and wondered when he would find the time or opportunity.

"Mrs. Dover hates dealing with the cold here in New York. Too bad, they miss all the best parties of the season." Father picked up one of the books Kingsley had stacked on a nearby table, and began flipping through the pages.

"Aren't they usually home for Christmas?" Kingsley asked. He seemed to recall attending at least one holiday party at the Dovers' home on Fifth Avenue.

"Usually, but by mid-January, they sail south." Father snapped the book closed and placed it on the table with the others Kingsley had gathered for his research.

"I can see the advantages of visiting Italy in winter." Kingsley wasn't a fan of ice, snow, and cold. It tended to wreak havoc with plumbing and pipes. He wondered if there were a way to create insulation for pipes that was more efficient than the current process. It was worth considering.

"Don't let your mother hear you say such things," Father said, interrupting his thoughts. "Winter season in New York is ritual for her."

"Humm, yes, so I know." Kingsley didn't need to be reminded. Edith Goddard preferred to spend the summer months with her seven children at their home on the Hudson River, or dashing off to spend time in Newport with one friend or another, but come the first of October she was back in New York, busily filling her calendar with every tea, luncheon, party, and ball that society could present. At least twice a month during the winter season, their New York mansion was filled to overflowing with flowers, fancy foods, and Edith's endless list of friends. Edith Goddard had once been a singer and actress and it seemed the art of performance was still in her blood. She may have left the theatre to marry George Goddard, but she never lost her desire for well-staged presentation.

"Are you going out to Riverwood this weekend?" Kingsley asked as he flipped to another page in the book containing more diagrams of Roman engineering. Fascinating stuff. However, a little assistance with the technical translations might prove helpful. He wondered if Mother's new Italian governess could provide such assistance.

"Leaving late Thursday afternoon. Care to join me?" Father settled into the big, comfy armchair next to his reading desk.

Kingsley was hoping his father would ask. As much as he liked being off on his own, away from the family, he hated traveling alone. Of

23

course, he always took his valet with him, but traveling with a servant was still very much like traveling alone. The cultural separation between them did not allow for amicable conversation. "Thursday works for me. I'll meet you here at the house and we can ride to the train station together."

"Sounds like a plan. Will you be attending Vanderbilts' party tomorrow?"

Kingsley gave his father a questioning look, surprised he had even asked. "I wasn't planning on it. I don't see any reason why I should." Ever since Alva Vanderbilt had refused to allow Consuelo to marry Kingsley, he had avoided the family and the exclusive society they represented. Mrs. Vanderbilt had made it clear his family wasn't good enough for her precious, only daughter. Though Alva came from a respected Southern family, her father had lost most of their wealth in the War Between the States. Even her husband's wealth was only three generations old, as opposed to Kingsley, whose great-grandfather was the initial source of the Goddard family fortune.

"They're celebrating Winston Montgomery's return from England," Father reminded him. "I would think you would at least want to see your old friend from college." Father picked up a pipe from his desk and began to pack it with tobacco. While Kingsley didn't smoke, he still held a childhood affection for the scent of his father's pipe.

"I'm sure I'll see him at the club. I doubt he's any more excited to attend a musical recital than I would be." Musicals, teas, and endless dinner parties were not Kingsley's idea of stimulating entertainment. He much preferred academic salons, or even the opera. Unlike most of his peers, he actually enjoyed listening to a well-produced opera from start to finish, instead of merely dropping in to make an appearance and then head off to one or another of the many after- theater parties.

Shuffling through the collection of books he had gathered on the table, Kingsley set aside three of them, including the one in Italian. The rest he returned to the shelves where he had found them.

Father eyed him with a look of concern. "Do you plan to avoid society forever?"

Shoving the final book into its slot, Kingsley replied. "Society, as you say, has no need for me, and I certainly have no need for them."

"Balderdash! You need to find a wife. Where else can you find a woman of the proper breeding and education?"

"You didn't need society to supply you with a perfectly lovely wife, why should I?" Although Kingsley was referring to the fact that his mother was once a stage actress, and for a time had not been accepted in the inner circles of society, he also hoped his father knew he meant no disrespect. He loved his mother and admired the closeness his parents shared. "If I could find a woman such as Mother, I would be well off indeed."

Father nodded with a look of affection as he puffed on his pipe. "Indeed, there are few like your mother. But let me caution you against turning your back on society. You never know when you may need such connections. Wasn't that how you met Max Branson? At Slone's house party last summer?"

"I don't deny I have benefited from my social connections, however, if nothing else, society has taught me how to pick and choose. For that, I suppose, I am grateful."

As a younger man, it seemed his confidence had depended upon the prevailing winds of social acceptance. Being a man of wealth was not a guarantee of confidence. When Alva Vanderbilt had set him down with her harsh rejection of his proposal to marry her daughter, his confidence had taken a significant blow. For a while, he had gone into hiding, basically avoiding any social situation where he risked being the blunt of malicious gossip. He knew society had gotten word of Mrs. Vanderbilt's rejection, and there was nothing her group enjoyed more than the sharing of some sordid tale, especially at someone else's expense. The cost of making such a foolish mistake was exceedingly high, and Kingsley felt he had paid the price.

But he was over that now. Perhaps, as his father advised, it was time to shed his dislike for society and take advantage of his connections. After all, he was an independently wealthy man, on his way to becoming well-established in his chosen profession. It was time to put the slight of

Alva Vanderbilt behind him, where it belonged, and get on with living. However, as for finding a wife, in that regards, he was in no hurry. Having just turned twenty-five, he figured he still had plenty of time before he was no longer considered a good catch within his set.

Kingsley began arranging the reference books and sketches he was working with as he prepared to settle in for a few hours of research and drafting of various ideas he had floating around in his head.

Father took another draw on his pipe, and then stood, looking as if he was about to leave. "So it's settled. We'll meet here Thursday afternoon and travel to Riverwood together. Will four o'clock work for you?"

"Perfect. I'll see you then. Now, if you will excuse me, I need to do some research if I am to be ready for my meeting with Branson later this week." Kingsley watched his father exit the room, grateful for the silence filled only by the ticking of the clock. It would have been rude to begin his research while his father was in the room, and once he began to work, he didn't like to be disturbed.

CHAPTER 3

Dressed for dinner, Kingsley entered the sunny drawing room of the family's summer home at Riverwood, and approached his mother. "Hello, Mother. You're looking well as always." He had arrived an hour or so earlier with Father, and had taken time to refresh after their train ride out from Tarrytown. Situated on a stunning piece of property overlooking the Hudson River, Riverwood had been the Goddards' summer home since Kingsley had turned fifteen.

Mother offered her cheek to receive his kiss. His father, it seemed, was still busy elsewhere. "Kingsley, my dearest, what a joy to see you. I had feared you were going to stay away all summer."

"You've only been here for a few weeks, I would hardly consider that all summer." Kingsley took a seat and smiled indulgingly at his mother.

Being the eldest of her seven children, and the first to leave the nest, she consistently reminded him how much he was missed whenever he was gone. While he was away at college, she had written him twice weekly, her letters filled with stories of the various functions she had attended and what his younger siblings were doing without him. Always, they ended with a line saying how much she missed him and looked forward to seeing him again soon. With such unceasing pressure, it was hard to disappoint her and stay away for too long before he was induced to make another visit home.

"How long can I hope to enjoy your company this time?" Mother asked.

"I've only just arrived. Are you already worried about when I will leave?" Kingsley teased.

"That is not what I meant, and you know it. Are you staying for the summer or only the weekend?" A crystal goblet of water sat on the table next to her chair, and she picked it up to take a sip. Throughout the summer months, Mother often had a glass of water or lemonade nearby. She claimed it helped to keep the body temperatures regulated.

"I'm not sure. That depends on how soon Mr. Branson needs me back at work. I've been working with him on his new project for the Newport resort. They're thinking of installing swimming baths similar to ones used in Rome, but these will be much larger. Bailey's Beach is planning to build the largest privately-owned saltwater swimming complex on the East Coast."

"Swimming baths? I've never heard of such a thing." Mother held her water glass in mid-air with an astonished look upon her face.

"Not surprising. They're a new idea, though based on a very old concept. Everything old becomes new again, sooner or later," Kingsley good-naturedly informed his mother. "Out in San Francisco, Adolph Sutro has already built something similar. I'm thinking of going out there to visit his facility later this year."

"Sounds like nonsense to me. Is this why you need to improve your Italian?" Mother inquired, setting down her glass. "Father told me you're reading Italian text books again."

"Quite right. I understand you've recently found a new Italian governess for the children. Is she any good?" Thinking his mother's drink looked refreshing, Kingsley went over to the sidebar that held a large pitcher of iced water to get a glass for himself.

"Marvelous. I couldn't be happier. She has the younger ones performing plays in Italian to keep us amused. They're really quite good."

"Plays in Italian? Surely, that puts her in your good graces. Perhaps tomorrow I should watch their lessons and see for myself if she's as good as you say." Before leaving the bar, Kingsley drank half his water and then poured a bit more to top it off.

"You won't be disappointed," Mother assured him. Once Kingsley had returned to his seat, she asked him, "So when are you planning a trip out to California?"

"California?" Father asked, stepping into the room.

"Yes, I was just telling Mother about the saltwater swimming pools Sutro built out in San Francisco. They're the largest in America. I was thinking I might take a trip in September to see them myself. I understand it's one of the nicest months out there."

"So soon? You've only just arrived." Mother looked dismayed.

"Mother, it's weeks away. Nearly the end of summer. I don't think you need to start missing me before I've gone." It wasn't yet July. Kingsley didn't plan to stay for the whole week, much less the whole summer. He had work to do back in New York.

"You make it sound as if you like this work," Father said with a note of pride.

"Yes, very much," Kingsley replied.

"I'm happy for you. Every man should like what he does. As for your mother, she would have you here year-round if it was up to her," Father said, patting his wife's hand.

"Except when she's busy attending teas, and parties, or hosting them herself," Kingsley reminded them.

"I like to keep busy. It's good for the soul," Mother said with a flare of drama.

"Will Jayson be joining us this weekend?" Kingsley asked, referring to his next younger brother. Jayson was in his last year of university and much like other young men his age, tended to prefer the company of his peers over his family, which was fine with Kingsley. His younger brother was one of those overly loud, boisterous, self-indulgent young men who gave their social class a bad reputation.

"He promised to be here by Saturday evening," Mother stated with confidence. "He knows I expect a full house for Sunday dinner. The children are going to perform their latest play for us."

"The boy will find the time, if he knows what's best," Father stated firmly.

Mother gave Father one of those pointed looks that showed she disliked his comment. "Everyone except the twins will be joining us for dinner tonight. Dina and Sandra still insist they're perfectly happy taking their meals in the nursery."

By everyone, Kingsley expected his mother was referring to the rest of his siblings still at home: Vivien, Howard and Helen. He wasn't surprised to hear Claudine and Cassandra preferred their own company over anyone else. Often, he had noted, the twins acted as if no one else was in the room. When Kingsley did take time to sit with his youngest sisters, he often felt slightly unnerved at how they tended to finish each other's sentences. Hopefully, they would overcome their need to limit their companionship by the time they were expected to make their debut. If not, they would have Mother in a fit over how to handle them. Still, he had to admire a woman who could give birth to twins and look as good as Edith Goddard. His mother called it the hardest year of her life. It had taken her months to get her figure back, but with determination and tenacity, she was able to still wear her ball gowns as before.

"I'm sure I'll see the twins tomorrow, that's soon enough. I'm thinking of sitting in to observe their lesson. What time do they meet with the Italian governess?" Kingsley asked.

"First thing in the morning. I believe they start right after breakfast. These days, since they're rehearsing for their performance, Miss Lucci often has them both before and after lunch time," Mother informed him. "I don't mind since it keeps them occupied. But after lunch, when the days are warm, they're much too restless to be any good at Italian lessons. Young ones must be allowed to play. It is summer, you know."

"I may not make it for all of the lesson, but I'll be sure to catch at least part of it." It sounded to Kingsley as if Miss Lucci was a bit of a taskmaster, keeping his younger siblings half the day to study Italian. It made him wonder how easy she would be to work with if he decided he wanted use her as a tutor, or more precisely, as a translator. Certain he'd find out soon enough, he set the matter aside for the rest of the evening.

Since he hadn't seen his mother in nearly a month, she spent much of their dinner hour regaling him with news and gossip about their neighbors on the Hudson and friends who had come to visit from New York. It gave him very little time to worry about old Italian textbooks or stern foreign governesses.

~*~

Kingsley stood just outside the doorway to the classroom, not wishing to be seen while he quietly observed his younger siblings and their teacher. For some reason, he had expected the governess to be an older, rounder, matronly type of woman; not the petite, slender, young beauty he found laughing happily with his younger brothers and sisters. Her mahogany brown hair was pulled back in a neat, stylish bun, and her dark brown eyes held a twinkle of merriment.

While he typically paid little attention to what women wore, surely he would have remembered if any of his governesses had looked as good as Miss Lucci did in her starched white blouse and navy blue skirt. As he recalled, his governesses had preferred gray and black clothing that made them appear as shapeless as feed sacks. But not Miss Lucci.

Shapely and pretty, she was far removed from any governess he had ever known before, and impressed him as being well-proportioned for a woman of her height. Since she stood nearly as tall as his sister Vivien, that still put her a good five or six inches shorter than himself. And while women in general seemed to compete for how tightly they could pull in their waists, Miss Lucci didn't appear to be tightly corseted. If anything, her stays seemed much more relaxed than current fashion dictated. He probably shouldn't be making such assessments on a woman he hadn't yet met, but his engineering mind seemed fixated on evaluating her form much the same way he'd evaluate a set of blueprints. A wayward line of thinking if ever there was one, but once his mind latched onto an idea there was no stopping until he came to a reasonable resolution, and his assessment of Miss Lucci was that she was reasonably well-proportioned for her height and width.

Darn, if he wasn't a bit envious of his younger siblings.

31

Not wishing to interrupt her lesson, Kingsley leaned against the door jam to watch for a while. From what he could understand, it seemed they were rehearsing lines from a play about a shoemaker and the elves who helped him while he slept each night.

It wasn't long before his brother Howard spied him lounging in the doorway and announced his presence, causing his siblings to stop what they were doing and clamber for his attention. Since he had obviously interrupted their studies, Kingsley attempted to make amends by making a formal introduction to the governess.

"Excuse me. Allow me to introduce myself. I'm Kingsley Goddard. As you may have guessed, your students are my siblings."

"Signore Kingsley," the governess gave him a smiling nod. "I'm Miss Lucci. It's a pleasure to meet you. Mrs. Goddard informed me you might come to watch our studies." For one brief second, her smile shined bright, but as quickly as it had appeared, it faded, replaced with the type of somber look he'd seen many times before on the strict and proper governesses of his youth. He hoped she was kinder to his siblings than the ones he had known as a child.

"Stay with us, Kingsley," Howard yapped, tugging at his sleeve. "Stay and watch us practice our play."

"It's the shoemaker and his elves." Claudine and Cassandra spoke almost in unison, except one had spoken in Italian, and the other in English.

"I'm the shoemaker," Howard stated proudly.

"I'm the shoemaker's wife," Vivien chimed in. "In case you're wondering."

"Are you going to stay and watch?" Helen asked. "I'm the head elf."

"I would like to, if it's not an imposition," Kingsley said, addressing the governess.

Miss Lucci took an appraising look at her students before she answered. "I prefer to keep these rehearsals private so the play will be polished and perhaps more entertaining when presented, you understand, but I don't suppose it will hurt if you to stay for a little while."

32

Kingsley understood her hesitation. It was probably hard enough to keep his younger brother and sisters focused on their studies. Learning Italian couldn't be all that fun. Add an audience and they were sure to become either shy or rambunctious.

"Should we start at the beginning, Miss Lucci?" Howard asked. "That's where I have the most lines," he explained to Kingsley.

"*Per favore, parla italiano*," Miss Lucci gently admonished her pupil. *Please, speak Italian.*

Looking appropriately chastised, Howard duly repeated what he had said in Italian, although at a somewhat slower pace.

"As much as possible, I ask my students to only speak Italian. I believe it increases their learning by staying immersed in the language," Miss Lucci explained to Kingsley in English.

"*Capisco*," Kingsley replied, letting her know he understood.

"Let us pick up where we were," Miss Lucci said, resuming her native language, and motioning for her students to return to their places. From Howard's groan of disappointment Kingsley figured that meant they would not be going back to the beginning as his brother had requested.

The front of the classroom was set up as their stage and the ones not in the scene stood off to the left, awaiting their cue. Kingsley took a seat near the back of the room and settled in to watch his siblings. Howard and Vivien stood off stage as Helen and the twins took their places on the makeshift stage. With a nod from Miss Lucci, Helen, as head elf, began calling out instructions to the twins, which Dina and Sandra then repeated. Kingsley surmised they were playing a scene in which the elves had slipped into the shoemaker's workshop during the night to secretly make his shoes.

"Stitch the leather, good and tight," called out Helen in Italian as she moved her hands in stitching motion.

"Stitch the leather, good and tight," repeated Dina and Sandra as one, following Helen's actions.

"Polish the leather, shiny and bright," Helen said her line while swiping her hands through the air.

33

"Polish the leather, shiny and bright." Again, the twins mimicked their older sister's lines and actions.

Due to turn ten in a few months, the twins were nearly six years younger than Helen, their next older sibling. After Helen was born, their mother had thought she was done having babies, and was both shocked and delighted when she became pregnant again. After such a delay, she had never guessed she would have another child, much less twins.

As he watched his siblings run through their lines, Kingsley could easily see the benefit of this simple play as a learning tool. It allowed the younger twins to learn from Helen, and gave her a sense of leadership as the head elf. Seeing their enthusiasm, Kingsley had to chuckle. They made such endearing elves. It seemed their mother's talent for acting was in their blood. If that were true, it must have bypassed him. The idea of performing in front of an audience, even if it were only his family, didn't appeal to him. He was much more comfortable sitting alone in a room examining engineering diagrams and designing ways to make improvements.

While watching his younger siblings learn their parts wasn't exactly exciting, watching Miss Lucci was much more interesting than Kingsley had anticipated. Her melodious accent was enticingly soothing as she gently instructed Howard and his sisters through their lines, patiently waiting when they hesitated or stumbled over words they couldn't remember.

It was nearing noon when Kingsley noticed a nursemaid dressed in a dull grey uniform step into the room. Apparently, she was expected. Miss Lucci quickly brought her students to a stopping point and dismissed them for lunch.

"Will you join us for lunch?" Howard asked Kingsley as he headed for the door ahead of his sisters.

"Not today. Mother's waiting for me. Maybe another time." He ruffed a hand through his younger brother's hair. The children of the house typically took their lunch in the small family dining room next to the courtyard gardens while Kingsley was expected to dine in the larger, formal dining room with his mother and father. "First I would like to speak to Miss Lucci." Turning to her, he added, "If you can spare the time?"

"Certainly, Signore Kingsley," Miss Lucci answered sweetly.

~~~

Normally, Anna Maria felt serenely confident in her role as governess and master of the classroom, but currently, she was dealing with a whole new set of emotions she had not expected upon waking this morning. The moment Signore Kingsley walked into her domain, her thoughts had gone to a place completely off limits to a proper governess. Especially a God fearing Christian woman such as herself. A man's thighs and the cut of his trousers should not be foremost in her mind upon meeting her employer's son for the first time, or how his dark, wavy hair perfectly framed his classically handsome features, and yet, those were the very thoughts vying for her attention.

Fully aware of how truly improper such thoughts were, she steeled herself to treat Signore Kingsley with proper, professional manners as befitting her station in his family home. Drawing on the same determination that had brought Anna Maria to America, it took her only seconds to disregard the fact that Signore Kingsley's smile set her heart racing. Maintaining detached professionalism was much preferred over allowing wanton desire to have its way. With skilled determination, she had pushed on to complete the morning's lesson, even though every fiber of her being was acutely aware of Signore Kingsley's watchful eyes.

Once the children had departed with the nursery maid, Signore Kingsley turned to her. "I expect you're anxious to get to your lunch, and my parents will be waiting for me, so I'll make this brief. I'm doing research on the designs of Roman baths and have found an excellent reference book written in Italian. I studied Italian some years ago, but I've become rusty and could use some help with some of the more technical aspects of the translations. I'm wondering if you can provide your assistance."

His request seemed perfectly appropriate, inspired as it was by a need to further his professional education, rather than from a personal interest.

A slight feeling of relief rolled through Anna Maria. She could do this.

Still, she wondered how much Italian Signore Kingsley knew since the idea of teaching a grown man a new language was not exactly what she had in mind when she became a governess for Mrs. Goddard. "I'm certainly willing to try. While I'm not sure what technical terms you may be working with, I'm sure I can help make sense of the translation for you."

"Excellent. I'm sure it will take much longer if I try to attempt it on my own. You speak English much better than I speak Italian."

"I also speak Italian much better than I speak English," Anna Maria replied, proud of her heritage.

"That's why I need your lessons. I already speak perfectly good English, I need to improve my Italian." Was it her imagination, or did Signore Kingsley seem a bit nervous?

That was understandable. Anna felt a bit nervous herself. There was something about this particularly handsome man that set her on edge. However, since coming to work for Mrs. Goddard, Anna made it a rule not to get overly attached, or overly friendly, with any members of the family she worked for. That rule had been firmly established the minute she'd been told by Mrs. Dover that her services were no longer needed and Mrs. Goddard had implied she would unduly influence young Howard with her feminine wiles.

Returning to the reason Signore Kingsley had sought her services, Anna asked, "Since I spend a good portion of each day with your siblings, when do you propose we meet?"

"If you're available, I would prefer late afternoon or evenings. Let's say four or five o'clock. Will that work for you?" he asked with an air of expectancy, as if knowing his request could not be refused.

"Certainly." It wasn't as if she had much say in the matter. While it was still a reasonable hour, she wasn't sure she liked the idea of spending her evenings with her employer's eldest son. It seemed slightly improper. "Will we be using this classroom?" she asked, thinking he looked a bit out of place in the youthful surroundings.

"I would prefer the library, if you don't mind. I left the upstairs nursery some years ago and do not wish to return to the territory of my younger brother and sisters."

"Of course, as you wish." She hoped he planned to keep the pocket doors of the library pushed open to avoid the appearance of impropriety.

"If it bothers you, we can keep the pocket doors open," Signore Kingsley said with a wolfish grin.

It riled Anna to know her thoughts were so transparent—she was going to need to work on that—and simply nodded her head in agreement.

"So, tell me, what do you do when you're not teaching my siblings Italian?" Signore Kingsley gestured toward the door and began to guide her out of the room toward the main staircase. Normally, she would use the back stairs to head down to the servants' hall to take her lunch, but since she was with her employer's son, she followed his lead.

"I use my time to prepare their lessons," she informed him. Although she wasn't a servant with daily chores, Anna Maria dedicated several hours each day outside the classroom making notes on the children's progress, going over their worksheets, and preparing lesson plans for the next day.

"Yes, of course, I'm sure you're quite dedicated to your duties. However, you must have some free time of your own." They had reached the top of the stairs and he reached out his hand to assist her as they stepped down.

Anna hesitated for a moment, but quickly chided herself for being silly. He was only being polite, she need not read more into his gesture than was intended. "Your family library holds an impressive collection of books, and I often use my time to read in an effort to learn more about the subjects I plan to teach my students," she said as she accepted his arm.

Though she thought of them as her students, at age nineteen and seventeen, Miss Vivien and Mr. Howard hardly seemed like children anymore. When she had first come to work at Riverwood, she had been somewhat surprised to discover the age of Mrs. Goddard's children.

Whereas Mrs. Dover's oldest son had only been thirteen, and the youngest five, Mrs. Goddard's children ranged in age from nineteen to nine years old. Another surprising discovery was when she learned all of Mrs. Goddard's children were still assigned to bedrooms on the nursery floor, and took their lessons together. All except the two oldest sons, Signore Kingsley and Mister Jayson, who had already moved out of the house.

But who was she to question the ways of her employer. The position paid well enough and provided her a comfortable place to stay.

Anna Maria suspected Miss Vivien and Mister Howard would not remain in the classroom much longer, certainly not longer than the end of summer. Most everyone in the family expected Miss Vivien would be married within the year, and Mr. Howard would return to an apartment at the university at the end of summer, leaving only the three youngest girls still at home. It made her wonder how much longer they would need her services, and if once again, she would someday soon find herself handed off to yet another wealthy family to teach a new set of children.

"I suppose being out here on the Hudson, away from the city, leaves very little in the area of entertainment," Signore Kingsley stated.

"I tend to stay on the property. I've no interest in exploring on my own." *Nor the means.* It wasn't as if she had access to a horse and carriage at her disposal, or excess funds to spend on amusements. Something the Goddard family surely took for granted.

"Perhaps, later, if you're available, I can show you around the grounds. A nice walk and some fresh air seems a pleasant activity for this fine afternoon. And the local village has some fine shops and pubs."

Her first reaction was to decline. She wasn't accustomed to being in the company of a family member outside of the classroom. "I'm not really sure if I should, considering my schedule." *Or if that's a good idea.*

"Of course, if you're too busy, we can always put it off for another day," Signore Kingsley offered, providing Anna with an opportunity to decline.

"Yes, perhaps that would be better. I had planned to use this afternoon to prepare for the next play I hope to teach the children. They will be performing The Shoemaker and The Elves this Sunday for the family and I want to be sure I have a new play waiting for them to learn."

They had reached the bottom of the stairs and she drew her hand back to her side. Time for them to go their separate ways.

"Will they have no rest between assignments?" Signore Kingsley asked as he turned to face her, showing no signs of an imminent departure.

"A day or two at most, but I feel it's best to keep them thinking in Italian if they are to really know the language."

"A serious taskmaster, I see. I hope I can live up to your standards." He spoke with a jesting smile.

Returning his smile, she replied, "That is yet to be seen, Signore Kingsley, but you are correct, I do have an exacting manner."

"I will do my best to impress you."

"I expect you will." She doubted he would have any problem in that regard. The politeness and attention he showed her, coupled with his distinguished good looks, had already made a rather significant impression on her. As tempting as it was to linger in his company, his parents were expecting him to join them for lunch, and she needed to be on her way. "Well, then, until our appointed hour, good day to you, sir."

"Good day to you, Miss Lucci."

Turning on her heel, she headed off toward the kitchen. She didn't need to look back to know he was watching as she walked away. After she had turned the corner and was out of sight, she released a little sigh. Their initial meeting had gone better than she had expected, but his attentions also left her slightly a-flutter, which she did not enjoy. She wasn't quite sure how she should handle Signore Kingsley, especially if his interest went beyond simply improving his Italian as he proclaimed.

Based on her brief time in his company, Anna judged Signore Kingsley as a scholarly type, more at ease around books and blueprints than racehorses and stock markets. But that didn't mean he was lacking in charm. After her time in London, his serious demeanor was much

39

more appealing than the empty-minded braggarts she had seen gathered outside London's pubs. They were harmless sorts of men, she supposed, but they reminded her too much of her father. Men like that expected those around them to follow their lead and do as they were told. Anna much preferred the serious study partners she had met through her brother Carlo at their London flat.

Handsome, polished and sophisticated, as one would expect from a man born to money, Signore Kingsley stood several inches taller than Anna with dark, wavy hair worn longer than was currently in style. Several times during their conversation, she had felt uneasily mesmerized by his piercing, dark blue eyes, and had to stop herself from staring. His strong angular jaw, pronounced cheekbones and aristocratic nose all spoke of good breeding. He was certainly attractive enough to catch a woman's eye. He had definitely caught hers. What could she say? She liked good-looking men, and Signore Kingsley was a good-looking man. Maybe not overly handsome, but being nice and well-mannered added a measure of appeal to any man.

Signore Kingsley seemed nice enough, but those of the wealthy class often did until you got to know them better. As Anna Maria has already learned, rich men and women cared little for the working class and those they employed to maintain their lifestyle. After being handed off from one family to another without a word of consideration, she harbored a certain level of resentment for the rich and all they represented, including their power over her, and their condescending ways. If they wanted something, they believed they could simply buy it, including people's lives. They had ungodly big houses, ridiculously expensive wardrobes, and wasted vast qualities of food. The idea of living simply so others could simply live seemed outside their way of thinking.

Still, it didn't escape her notice that nearly everything in her life resulted from her employment by a rich family. Because of her rich employers, she had moved to America. Thanks to the Goddards, and the Dovers before them, she had a roof over her head, a bed to sleep in, and food to eat. Sometimes, they even supplied the dresses she wore. But the one thing they could neither give nor take was her love of learning and her desire to share her knowledge with others. Her personality, her spirit, her sense of morals, these were all hers, and she would guard them well against the greedy hands of the rich.

CHAPTER 4

S hortly before the appointed hour, Kingsley took his reference books to the library and began to set up a workspace on one of the reading tables in the middle of the room. Nearly two stories high, the library filled the northwest corner of the house and held almost as many books as Father kept at their Fifth Avenue mansion. Many of them were stored behind locked, glass-fronted cabinets to protect them from dampness or cold. Setting aside the others he had brought with him in a stack, he pulled out the one written in Italian in anticipation of Miss Lucci's arrival.

After conferring with Mother regarding her daily schedule, he had decided five o'clock would be a suitable time for his first session with Miss Lucci, and had sent word for her to meet him in the library. He didn't really think of it as a lesson. This was more of an opportunity for him to refresh his Italian while they worked together to translate the Italian textbook. He found the idea of working side-by-side with Miss Lucci rather appealing, considering all his prior teachers had been men. Never before had he thought to collaborate with a woman, and he was rather looking forward to seeing how well their personalities fit.

He had just finished organizing his supply of pencils and paper when she walked into the room. Still dressed in the blouse and skirt from this morning, she looked as fresh and lovely as she had hours ago. One would never guess she had spent her morning in the classroom directing his younger brother and sisters. If he were required to spend the day with his siblings, he was sure it would leave him looking haggard and exhausted. But not Miss Lucci. From what he had seen, she seemed to enjoy their company.

"Right on time. I like that in a woman." Kingsley said, standing as she walked into the room.

"Do you not also appreciate promptness in a man?" she asked as she came forward, leaving the pocket doors open as they had agreed.

He was sorely tempted to go and close the doors, as was usual for him when working on his research, but in consideration of their earlier discussion, he respected her preference for propriety.

Kingsley held out a chair for her to take a seat at the table where they would be working. "Of course, I appreciate promptness in a man, it's just that, well women are known . . ."

"Known for what?" she asked with a raised brow as she smoothed her skirts and sat down.

"For their lack of punctuality, of course. Although, actually, I'm speaking from my experiences in social situations. I'll admit, this is my first time engaging in business with a woman." He took the chair next to her and brought the textbook between them on the table.

"Is that what we're doing? Engaging in business? I had thought this was an Italian lesson," she said, with a delightfully perplexed look.

"In a manner, I would say this is business. We're working together to translate a resource book. What else would you call it?"

"You're quite right. I suppose we should get right to work, don't you agree? Have you made much of an attempt to translate the book on your own yet?" she asked, pulling the book closer.

"I've only skimmed through it enough to see that it's of interest to me. Since I knew I would need help with the translation, I've focused my attention on the other books I've gathered on this subject."

"Are there a lot of books written about the Roman baths?" she asked, flipping through the first few pages of the book.

"The others are about mechanical engineering and the use of industrial plumbing, which is what I need to research for my upcoming

43

project. I'm working with Mr. Branson to secure a contract with the Bailey Beach Resort to build some extensive saltwater swimming pools." Kingsley was proud to have a part in this particular commission. It promised to be both lucrative and highly creative. Engineering designs would be needed for both the fresh and salt water plumbing fixtures, and he was anxious to show he was worthy of the task.

"If the resort is at the beach, why do they need swimming pools? Can't they just go into the ocean?" It was a perfectly reasonable question, but Miss Lucci's sweetly confused look had him smiling.

Still, he answered her in all seriousness. "The shoreline at that location is extremely rocky, making the swimming experience not very pleasant. Since the resort is exclusive to a limited membership, they want to make it as nice as possible."

"I see. We wouldn't want them to stub their little toes when the rich go out to play."

Though her tone sounded playful, her remark seemed slightly judgmental. Kingsley chose to ignore it and focus on the task at hand. "How do you suggest we do this?" he said, gesturing at the book.

"I understand you have some familiarity with Italian, am I correct?"

"*Corretta.*"

"In that case, since I understand you also wish to improve your Italian, I recommend you read a page or two, first in Italian and then translated into English. I'll assist you and make corrections as needed."

"That seems like a rather slow way to go through the material." The reference book was nearly five hundred pages long, and although there were several diagrams included in the text, her process seemed overly tedious.

"I only need you to do this until I can get a feeling for how much you know. Then we can decide how much help you need and how to proceed."

He liked her logic. "Sounds fair enough."

He began reading the first page of the introduction in Italian, then converted what he had read into English as the author described the various types of architecture and engineering projects covered in the book. Surprisingly, the process worked much better than Kingsley had expected. He also realized his Italian was better than he had thought.

"I'm impressed, Signore Kingsley. Your Italian is much better than I had expected. This shouldn't be hard at all."

Not the best of compliments, but he understood her meaning. "*Grazie, Signorina* Lucci." Speaking in Italian, he continued, "Would you mind if we skip ahead to the section I'm most interested in?"

"Not at all. Let's get right to the point." She also left English behind, indicating they would now speak only in Italian. Apparently, he had proven a satisfactory level of competency.

They spent another thirty minutes working through the translation of the section describing the history of Roman architecture and how it pertained to the building of the extensive network of the Roman baths. While much of this introductory information focused on the cultural aspects behind the baths, he found it fascinating, and saw no reason to rush through the material, as he might have done if he were working on his own. Especially since he had such a pleasant and enjoyable tutor as *Signorina* Lucci.

The idea that communal bathing played such a significant role in Italy's ancient society was fascinating to a man raised in modern, modest times where even the touch of a hand was scrutinized for sexual overtones. As the author pointed out, *"though contemporary cultures see bathing as a very private activity conducted solely in the privacy of one's home, bathing in Rome was a communal activity, a time for neighbors to meet and socialize."* Still, when he compared their baths to the concept of going to the seashore to enjoy swimming in the ocean as part of an accepted social activity, perhaps they were not so very different after all. The bathing complex that the managers of the Bailey Resort intended to build wasn't so very different from the facilities created in Roman times.

Interestingly, as he read aloud about bathing and public baths, he felt no sense of embarrassment as he might have expected with a woman at his side. *Signorina* Lucci had such an air of pragmatic confidence, any thoughts of discomfort or awkwardness regarding the information seemed absurd.

As they continued to work through the material, Kingsley was impressed by how well their first session progressed. They seemed to fall into a comfortable association, not as teacher and student, but as two people who worked well together. Miss Lucci, it seemed, was as interested in the material as he was.

"I'm impressed by the depth of history and architectural detail presented here," Miss Lucci stated.

"I knew the book was going to be helpful," Kingsley offered. "It's why I've been so anxious to work on its translation. Working with you is giving it even greater meaning, considering your familiarity with the language and the land."

"I'm sure you could have done a fair job of understanding this on your own, but together, it's as if we . . ."

"Bring something to share?" Kingsley finished for her.

"Precisely. I doubt I would have ever thought to read a book like this, but working with you, seeing how excited you are, greatly improves this experience."

"It's as if we're both seeing it with fresh eyes."

"Yes, exactly," she said, her eyes shining bright. "Who knew Roman baths could be so interesting and innovative?"

Delighted by her response, Kingsley knew exactly what she meant. He wondered if this was what it was like for his younger twin sisters. Perhaps similar, but surely not the same. Dina and Sandra had spent their whole life together, even before they were born, whereas he had only just met Miss Lucci.

Kingsley was suddenly struck with the most vivid image of Miss Lucci stepping into a public bath, followed almost immediately by an image of her stepping out of the bath, dripping wet and nearly nude. To make matters worse, he found his gaze had traveled to an area slightly south of her chin, watching as her breasts rose and fell with her breath. Forcing his gaze back to her face, he cleared his throat. It had suddenly gone dry.

"Everything all right?" Miss Lucci asked, naively unaware of his improper thoughts.

46

"Perfectly," he replied as he carefully set down the pencil he'd been holding in midair, his voice tighter than usual.

The clock on the wall struck the hour and Kingsley looked up. Six o'clock, where had the time gone? It felt as if they had just sat down together.

"My, how time flies. I'm tempted to ask you to stay longer, but I must leave to dress for dinner. If we continue on, I suspect I may lose track of time." *If not control of my thoughts.* "Mother frowns on being kept waiting."

"I understand completely. We should stop for the night."

Anxious to see her again, he asked, "Shall we meet again tomorrow to continue this work?"

"On a Saturday? I would think you have better ways to spend your time here in the country than translating an Italian text book." Miss Lucci replied.

Not likely. "Right. Tomorrow is Saturday. Not a good day to be cooped up in a classroom, although I suspect you will have my brother and sisters doing last minute practice for the performance on Sunday."

"Corretto! The children and I expect to spend most of the day preparing for their play. They're very excited to perform for your parents. You can always work on the text without me." She gathered up the notes they had taken and began organizing them into a neat little pile.

"I'd rather not." Following her lead, Kingsley placed the pencils, and penknife used to sharpen them, back in their holder. "I'd much prefer to wait until you're available." He had intended to return to New York with his father early Monday morning, but now he was beginning to rethink his plans. Anxious to continue working with Miss Lucci, he thought it best if he extended his stay into the following week. It was only because they had made such impressive progress with this first session, he told himself—discounting his momentary flash of fantasy— and he didn't want to lose the momentum.

Although Miss Lucci was charming and a pleasure to work with, he didn't want to read too much into their initial success. It could easily be that once they got to the more technical aspects of the material, he would find she was not up to the task. He didn't want to overestimate her abilities. That didn't seem prudent based on such limited evidence. And yet, he couldn't help but hope.

Miss Lucci looked uncertain. "If I can get away for an hour or two, I will let you know. What are your plans for tomorrow?"

"Breakfast with Mother, and then a ride along the river with Father. My brother Jayson may be arriving tomorrow evening, but I believe my afternoon is free."

"Perhaps I can find some time tomorrow afternoon if the children need a break from the play."

Kingsley allowed himself to smile, filled with expectation. "From what I have seen, I doubt you'll have any trouble telling my brother and sisters what to do."

"I don't believe I'm overly strict," Miss Lucci stated, sounding somewhat offended.

"Not at all. If anything, you have such a gentle manner, I feel Howard and the girls would gladly do your bidding just to please you."

A slight blush crept onto her cheeks. "I think you overestimate my influence on them. They were merely showing off because you were in the room, not to make me look good."

"That may have been part of it, but nevertheless, I have a feeling they're very devoted to you." He could certainly understand why. He was feeling much the same way.

"I think they're devoted to performing well for your parents. Your mother in particular. They want very much to impress her, knowing she was once an actress herself."

Kingsley wondered how Miss Lucci felt about his mother's previous profession. There were some who saw her early acting days as a blemish on her reputation, and snubbed her because of it. Regardless what the high and might Alva Vanderbilt or Caroline Astor may think of her past, being married to a wealthy man had a way of opening doors that might otherwise have been closed.

"Mother loves everything her children do," Kingsley assured her. "She'll clap the loudest and the longest, no matter how they perform."

"If she is not truly pleased, I think they will know. But enough, you must leave to prepare for dinner, and I am needed in the nursery to assist with the twins. I understand they are not dining with the family." Before he could assist her, she pushed back her chair from the table and stood.

Kingsley also stood. "As I'm sure you've noticed, they prefer to keep their own company."

"Yes, they're quite a pair." Her smiling eyes were a sure sign of her affection for his youngest sisters. "You mentioned your other brother is also expected to come home for the weekend?"

As they talked, they walked to the foyer outside the library.

"Jayson. Yes, if he can pull himself away from his friends. Being at university provides plenty of opportunities for distractions, but Mother made him promise he'll be here, so I expect he'll find a way to make it happen."

At the foot of the stairs, she paused to bid him good night.

Knowing it might be a day or two before they could spend time together was slightly disappointing. She was busy with her duties, as was he, but Kingsley still hoped he could persuade her to make time for him. "I look forward to seeing you tomorrow."

She raised a questioning brow.

"I expect my siblings will need at least some sort of break in their day," he argued, unwilling to allow an opportunity to see her again pass him by.

"Perhaps, Signore Kingsley, if I can find the time, but I'll make no promises."

"Perhaps is good enough for now."

"Good night, Signore Kingsley." She turned and headed toward the back of the house.

After watching her walk away, Kingsley returned to his room to dress for dinner, thinking how nice it would be if Miss Anna Maria Lucci could take dinner with him instead of with his sisters.

~*~

They had just finished the first course when Mother asked, "Kingsley, have you had a chance to meet Miss Lucci yet?"

"I did. I stopped by the classroom this morning to introduce myself and get a peek at her teaching style. We've had our first meeting to work on the reference book shortly before dinner. She's not at all what I expected," Kingsley replied, thinking how pleasantly surprised he had been to find a young and attractive governess instead of the older, more matronly types he had experienced in his youth.

"How do you mean?" Mother asked.

"She has some unusual methods for approaching the matter. I suppose I rather expected her to do the work for me, but she had me read and translate the material with very little assistance from her." Kingsley waited until everyone had been served their soup before taking a taste. It seemed Mother had found another splendid cook to replace the one they lost last Christmas.

"Were you able to do that?" Mother asked. She took a sip of the soup and smiled, undoubtedly pleased by the cook's talents.

"Better than I would have thought." He had expected to struggle through the translation, but it seemed he had retained more of the language than he had given himself credit for.

"That's why we like her," Howard interjected. "She acts as if we already know how to speak Italian and just need to practice."

"Does it work?" Kingsley's siblings didn't have nearly as much training in Italian as he, and he wondered how they were able to pick up the language so quickly.

"You saw for yourself how well we're doing with the play," Vivien offered.

"There must be some merit to her method," Father commented.

"As long as she keeps the children occupied, I'm happy," Mother said.

"But how do you know if it's doing any good?" Kingsley asked. "I mean, sure they can recite the lines of a play, but if Howard finds himself stranded in Rome, can he really use what he has learned, or will he be reduced to reciting lines about elves and little old shoemakers?"

In perfect Italian, Howard stated, "*Per favore, mi sa dire dove si trova la stazione ferroviaria? Devo prendere il treno alle quattordici per*

Venezia." Please, can you tell me how to get to the train station? I must catch the four o'clock train to Venice.

Kingsley laughed. *"Touché."*

"Well, I guess that answers that question," Father stated. "Kingsley, we're still set to go riding tomorrow, correct? Does nine o'clock work for you?" Father took a final spoonful of soup and sat back on his chair.

"Can you make it ten?" Mother asked. "I was hoping to eat breakfast with you both, and you know I hate to rise so early in the morning."

"Ten it is," Father agreed with a firm smile. "What are your plans for tomorrow?" He set down his wine glass and let the footman refill it.

"I plan to putter around the garden after breakfast. Bernice Dorvall is coming for tea in the afternoon," Mother said.

"Please, give her my regards if I don't see her," Father said. "I plan to head over to the village after lunch to pay a visit to Reverend Declan while I'm here."

"Can't that wait until Sunday, after services?" Mother asked. "I'm sure Bernice would love to see you."

"He's always too busy on Sundays," Father replied. "I'd rather not have to wait while everyone takes their fifteen minutes to discuss their views on the sermon before I can get a minute of his time. Besides, this isn't about religion. I plan to ask him how the hunting's been this season."

Kingsley could relate to Father's urgent desire to meet with Reverend Declan. He was known for his impatience when it came to waiting his turn. Kingsley was also anxious for his next meeting with Miss Lucci.

CHAPTER 5

Anna Maria stepped outside to enjoy the pleasant summer day and a few moments alone. She had spent the morning with the children going over their play and was pleased to have this break while her students enjoyed their lunch. It had been agreed that her students would also be given an hour of free time before they were scheduled to resume their final rehearsal for the day.

After grabbing a quick bite of meat pie from the servants' hall, she hurried to take advantage of what little time she had to enjoy the expansive gardens of the Goddard summer home. The park-like setting was breathtakingly beautiful, thanks to the gardeners employed by Mrs. Goddard. At least three of them were on the estate full-time, and additional help was employed whenever needed. It seemed Mrs. Goddard liked to keep disruptions at her summer home to a minimum to preserve the quiet serenity of the place, and arranged to have renovations done as quickly and efficiently as possible, both inside and out.

As Anna leisurely strolled down a path in one of the more mature, established gardens, enjoying the warm sunshine and fragrant scent of flowers, she briefly considered whether she should try to find Signore Kingsley to work on the translation of his book, but quickly rejected the idea. She would much rather use her limited free time enjoying the sunny day than staying cooped up in the library. She deserved a break as much as the children, and hopefully, after they finished their final rehearsal, she would still have time to meet with Signore Kingsley before the dinner hour.

If not, then, oh well, at least she hadn't promised. She had only said she would try to find time for him and his translation.

Thankfully, they worked well together. Although Signore Kingsley struck her as a man with very little patience for nonsense, he wasn't without a sense of humor, not in the least. There had been a number of times she had detected an underlining note of wit to his comments. Not that she was so inclined to nonsensical silliness herself, at least not when she was working as a governess for young impressionable children.

Society, it seemed, placed almost unnatural expectations upon a governess to act in a manner devoid of humor and joy. But teaching children should be a joyful and richly rewarding experience for both the tutor and the student.

Sometimes, when she'd been in London with her brother, they had enjoyed moments of unrestrained, frivolous laughter while they entertained his friends. No doubt, the distance from her father had contributed to her feeling of freedom to be herself. Working as a governess, such moments seemed so rare as to not exist at all, and there were times when she found herself wishing for those happier times.

Though she had willingly left home and moved halfway around the world, she wasn't looking for a husband. She didn't need a man to look after her. If anything, she had been the one looking after her brother in London, even though he was thirteen months older than she. Thankfully, since becoming a governess, she no longer relied on her father to provide for her well-being. His support had stopped the day she told him to stop shouting at her siblings.

While she wasn't in a hurry to get married, what Anna Maria really wanted most was a home of her own, with children of her own whom she could shower with loving approval. It would be nothing like the reign of terror her father inflicted upon his children. Instead, she dreamed of a large, noisy, Italian family that didn't always mind their manners or worry about being proper every hour of the day, especially at mealtimes. And she wouldn't have governesses or nursemaids tending to them while she sipped tea with women who ate too many cakes and spoke judgmentally about others who weren't in the room.

When she reached a shaded, tree-lined fork in the path, she stopped to choose a direction. She believed the path on her left would eventually lead her back to the house, while the one heading off to her right seemed to head toward the far side of the estate. Knowing she needed to return to the house, she was about to turn around and head back when the crunching sound of heavy boots traveling along the pea-graveled path reached her ears. Thinking it was one of the gardeners going about his business, she paused, hoping to have an opportunity to tell him how much she enjoyed his handiwork. As the man came into view, she realized it was Signore Kingsley. He was the last person she had expected to see, and yet, the sight of him, dressed in riding clothes, set her pulse racing. Taking a deep breath to calm her nerves, she noticed the path he walked on came from the direction of the stables.

Signore Kingsley was humming a cheery tune as he walked, seemingly without a care in the world, but stopped abruptly when he spied Anna, looking slightly embarrassed.

"Miss Lucci, what a surprise. I had no idea I would find you here." Looking around, he added, "Are you alone?"

"I just came out for a bit of fresh air. I'm expected back in the classroom soon for our final rehearsal of the play. You look as if you've been out riding." Which was an excellent reason for why she had not sought him out to continue the Italian translation.

"Quite right. Wonderful morning for a ride. Father and I went farther and rode longer than I expected. I wanted to stretch my legs, so I took this path through the garden on my way back to the house."

"It's a beautiful day for a walk. I couldn't resist myself."

"Yes, well, I'm not used to sitting a horse for quite so long, and needed to stretch my legs."

"Yes, so you said." It seemed Signore Kingsley was somewhat flustered, or perhaps nervous having come across her so unexpectedly. She wondered if it was because he'd been caught humming, or if there was some other reason for his skittish behavior.

54

"Since you're here, and so am I, would you mind if I walk with you?"

Anna smiled, charmed by Signore Kingsley's delightful lack of finesse. "I'd be happy to walk with you. I was just about to turn around and make my way back to the house."

"Excellent, I'll walk with you." Turning to take his place at her side, they fell into step as they meandered back toward the house. "I hadn't thought to ask you last night, but I was wondering what brought you to America? How long have you been here?" It seemed he had recovered from his initial bout of embarrassment.

"I was still living at home when I began working as a governess for the Dover family. I was hired by Mrs. Dover to tutor her children while they toured through Italy. A few months after we came to New York, Mrs. Dover heard your mother was in need of a new governess and I was asked to come and work for her." Anna was stretching the truth to say she was asked to change jobs, but to confess she had been handed off from one family to another without a word of consideration was too demeaning to admit.

She had left Italy in search of independence from her domineering father without resorting to marriage, especially to the man of his choosing. Resisting a shudder, she vividly recalled how her father had hoped she would marry Mr. Tarantino, the village butcher, but she had refused to consider his suit. Part of the reason her father had agreed to send her away with her brother to London was to stop their neighbors from constantly pointing out that his eldest daughter was still unmarried. In their small, remote village, there hadn't been a man within ten years of her age who held her interest. And certainly none who found her appealing. Italian men in her village didn't care for women who read books and spoke their mind.

Except now, as she had come to realize, instead of her father, she was dependent on her employer for her livelihood.

"Have you always wanted to be a governess?" Signore Kingsley asked.

My goodness, no! "I guess I never really thought about it." No little girl dreamed of taking care of other people's children, but coming from a working-class family, she had to do whatever it took to survive.

"I expect New York is quite different from Italy. Do you like it here?"

Anna paused, taking in the scent of a flowering jasmine vine as she thought about her answer. "It's different here, I agree, and in some ways better. There are many more opportunities here in America. Of course, I miss my family and my hometown, but I've also lived in London. Being away from home is not new to me, however that doesn't necessarily make it easier."

"Do you have any siblings?" He pinched off one of the jasmine blooms and handed it to her.

Accepting the sweet-smelling bloom, she twirled it beneath her nose. "There are five of us, my older brother, Carlo, me and my two sisters, and my youngest brother, Marco. I was with Carlo while he studied in London. That's where I learned English."

"But why America? Why leave the comfort of your family and home to come here?" Signore Kingsley persisted.

Anna took a moment to consider her answer. She wasn't inclined to reveal too much about herself. "Surely, for the same reason as most everyone else. To make a new life for myself."

"Forgive me if I'm being invasive, I don't mean to be rude, but that seems rather adventurous. I wouldn't expect a woman to travel alone to a foreign country."

She didn't see him as being rude, only persistent. "I wasn't alone. I was with the Dovers," she said as she tucked the sweet jasmine flower into the pocket of her skirt for safekeeping.

"I mean without your family, or a husband, or someone to watch over you."

His opinion on the subject wasn't unusual, especially coming from a man. "I spent a year in London without a husband. Why should coming to America be any different?" Although, of course, she knew the answer.

"But you were with your brother while you were in London, am I correct?"

"Yes, but—"

"So you were with family, someone to watch over you."

"What makes you think he was watching over me? Maybe I was watching over him." Which was partially true, considering she acted as both his housekeeper and conscience, since she was expected to report back to Pappa if Carlo had behaved inappropriately. Which she never had cause to do. Nor would she have unless Carlo did something truly bad, such as murder or mayhem. They both agreed, being away from Pappa's harsh rule was the best time of their lives.

"I've no doubt you're perfectly capable of taking care of yourself," he said with an appreciative smile.

"I'm glad you agree."

"I admire that about you."

Anna Maria didn't know quite how to respond. His compliment was perfectly harmless, and yet, Anna had the feeling Signore Kingsley was flirting with her. Regardless of what ideas he might have to the contrary, Anna had no intention of risking her position by flirting with Mrs. Goddard's eldest son.

"But still, wouldn't you prefer to let a man . . ." Signore Kingsley seemed to struggle to find the right words.

Not wishing to pursue his line of reasoning, Anna interrupted him. "If I needed a man to watch over me, I would have stayed at home. But I don't. Which is why I came to America." They had come to the edge of the garden and were about to cross over the terrace that led into the house. "Now if you'll excuse me, I need to get back to my classroom," she said, stepping onto the steps of the terrace.

Before she could slip away, he asked, "Will I see you later? To work on the translation?"

He sounded rather contrite, and Anna worried she had offended him, which wasn't her intention, at least not entirely. She simply didn't like it when men assumed every young woman needed the protection of a man to make her way in the world. Women were perfectly capable of taking care of themselves. They'd been doing it forever.

Turning back to face him, she said, "I'll let you know when we're done with our rehearsal. Where should I expect to find you?"

His lips curved up optimistically, making his features boyishly appealing. "If it's not too late, I'll be out here on the terrace. It's such a lovely day, I'd hate to spend it all inside."

Those were exactly her thoughts, which was why she had gone for the walk in the garden. And why he had found her walking alone.

"It shouldn't be that much longer, an hour or two at most. I'll look for you when we're done."

"Excellent. It'll give me time to change out of these dusty clothes and make myself presentable." His smile fell somewhere between apologetic for his appearance, and anxious for their next meeting. She hoped it wasn't the latter. An overly attentive employer was never a good idea for a working woman.

Besides, to her eyes, he already looked perfectly presentable in his well-fitting riding breeches and the royal blue coat that perfectly matched his smiling, friendly eyes. Not that she would ever state such a thing. She understood perfectly well how much rich folk liked to change from one outfit to another. It served as a way of showing off their extensive and expensive wardrobes, especially for the ladies. Still, wasn't it the male peacocks, with all their showy feathers, that tried to impress their potential mates. It was best not to be taken in by such fine attire.

They had nearly reached the entrance of the house when Anna Maria noticed Mrs. Goddard standing near the French doors. It looked as though she had been there for a while.

"Hello, Mother. Lovely day, wouldn't you agree?" Signore Kingsley greeted his mother.

"Quite lovely," Mrs. Goddard answered, before turning her attention to Anna. "Taking a break, Miss Lucci?"

"Mrs. Goddard, I was just enjoying a stroll through one of your lovely gardens when Signore Kingsley offered to walk with me back to the house."

"How very nice, but shouldn't you be up in the classroom with the children? They are preforming the play tomorrow, am I not right? I'm sure they're anxious to do their final run through." Though Mrs. Goddard sounded as if she were merely taking an interest in her children's studies, Anna heard the note of disapproval in her voice.

"I'm on my way there now. Signore Kingsley, thank you for your company." It was fairly apparent to Anna that Mrs. Goddard did not approve of her wasting time taking walks, especially not with her son. Making a quick departure, Anna headed off toward the back stairs that would take her to the classroom where she belonged.

~~~

Watching Miss Lucci walk away, Kingsley felt an emptiness beside him, and the strangest urge to hasten after her.

Before she was even out of the room, his mother asked, "Were you speaking with her about your lessons?"

Forcing his attention back to his mother, Kingsley gave an affirming nod. "The lessons? Um, yes, the translation of the Italian text is going quite well, better than I expected." He didn't think of his sessions with Miss Lucci as *lessons*. Nor did he care for the way his mother had addressed the governess, but he saw no reason to upset her by making an issue of the way she spoke to her servant. At this point, he figured it was best not to draw unnecessary attention to his feelings for Miss Lucci. He was still trying to figure out how to handle his attraction to a woman employed by his mother.

"I should hope so," Mother said tartly. "That's why we employ her. It's what we pay her for."

Though a governess, like the rest of the staff, wasn't paid all that much, people like his parents who employed them usually felt their wages were more than compensated by the food and lodging they provided. Agreeably, that might be true for most of the staff, especially those who worked to prepare and serve their meals, and keep the house and grounds well maintained, but Miss Lucci was an educated, well-traveled woman from a good family in Italy. Her father had the means to send her brother to London for a year so he could study at the university, and she had accompanied him. He didn't see Miss Lucci as just another one of the servants, but from Mother's tone, it was obvious she did.

"I can assure you, the service Miss Lucci provides me goes well beyond her duties as governess. Her assistance is invaluable," Kingsley informed his mother.

"Good to know. As long as you're happy, that's all that matters."

"How could I not be happy, being here with you at Riverwood?" Knowing such an answer would please his mother, he was rewarded with her contented smile. To change the subject, he asked, "Do you know if Father has returned from the stables yet?"

"I haven't seen him, and we're due to sit for lunch soon."

"I know he was planning to ride over to see Reverend Declan, but I thought that was later, after lunch." Summertime at Riverwood was meant to be leisurely, but regardless, Kingsley knew his mother preferred to maintain a formal schedule and keep herself occupied.

"That's what he said. And afterwards, I'm expecting Bernice Dorvall for tea."

"If I don't see her, please give her my best. Now if you will excuse me, I really must change out of these riding clothes."

Kingsley resumed humming his happy tune as he made his way up the main staircase to his bedroom to change. He hadn't expected to see Miss Lucci as he strolled through the garden on his way back to the house, but finding her there had been a pleasant surprise. That she should be walking in the section known as the lovers' garden—so named because of the tall shrubs and hedges that easily hid couples seeking a private place to meet—seemed an added bonus. He must have looked rather silly, coming upon her as he did, humming some ridiculous tune as if he hadn't a care in the world, and all the while, thinking of her. It had taken him a moment to regain his wits, or at least attempt to appear as though he were something less than a fool.

Kingsley liked spending time with Miss Lucci, not merely because she was smart and beautiful—a powerful combination—but because she challenged him to think in ways he hadn't before. Most women he knew did not value independence and education nearly as much as Miss Lucci did, especially her desire for independence. For women of high society, obtaining a financially-secure marriage was far more important than higher learning. But not Miss Lucci.

In his mind, those were precisely the qualities that set her so far above most women he knew.

After ringing for Jamison, his valet, Kingsley took a moment to consider which suit he wanted to wear. Should he appear scholarly and serious-minded—a man ready to get to work—or should he add a bit of flare to his outfit in an effort to impress Miss Lucci? She didn't appear like the type easily impressed by wealth or flamboyance, and in the end, he opted for a lightweight brown wool suit that seemed perfectly fitting for a sensible engineer intent on studying Italian architecture with a beautiful, compelling, and engaging tutor.

~*~

True to her word, Miss Lucci sought out Kingsley while he lounged on the terrace reading a trade journal. He had just finished an article on the wonders of the new Sutro baths serving the general public in San Francisco. Adolph Sutro had done everything within his power to ensure his project's success, and yet, as Kingsley read between the lines, it seemed Mr. Sutro had overbuilt for the location. Only seven thousand people had attended the opening ceremony last March, less than a third of the building's capacity, and on weekdays there were often fewer than a thousand guests using the enormous structure even during the busiest summer months. Kingsley made a mental note to confer with Mr. Branson regarding the size of the Bailey Beach Resort project to ensure they avoided this issue. Larger spaces meant constructing larger machinery needing greater maintenance, and an added greater expense for their client.

As soon as Miss Lucci stepped through the terrace doors, Kingsley set down his periodical and stood to greet her. While he was sorely tempted to look at his watch, he resisted lest she think he was keeping tabs on her, which he certainly wasn't. He appreciated her taking time from her busy schedule to assist him in his project. It didn't seem right to push too hard. From the angle of the sun, he suspected they had no more than an hour before he would need to excuse himself to prepare for dinner with his family, but he would take what he could get.

"Miss Lucci, I trust your final rehearsal went well," Kingsley said as she stepped out onto the terrace.

"As well as can be expected, I suppose. The children know their lines, there's no problem there, I only hope they don't experience stage fright when they perform for you and your parents."

"From what I know of my siblings, I believe you have little cause for concern. They have our mother's blood in them when it comes to performing. Give them an audience and they're happy to have the attention."

"Perhaps so, but keep in mind, this time they will be speaking Italian. Our brains can do strange things when we're not speaking our native language. One of them could forget their lines, or simply say the wrong thing, which would throw off the others."

He wondered if Miss Lucci had ever misspoken during their conversations. Her familiarity with the English language led him to believe she had no problem making herself understood. "I'm sure you've done all you can to ensure their success. At some point, you must trust their abilities. Shall we proceed to the library? Our work table is still set up from our last meeting. We can pick up where we left off."

"That's why I'm here," she said cheerfully, though he noted a look of weariness around her eyes.

Although he would regret losing this time with her, Kingsley worried if perhaps she should be allowed to take a break rather than hurry on to another assignment. "Are you sure you're not too tired?"

"Thank you, but I can assure you, I'm perfectly fine. I suspect we only have an hour at most. I'm happy to use this time to assist you."

He wondered if that meant she enjoyed his company as much as he did hers. Or if she were just being kind because, as a governess, it was expected of her. Either way, he wasn't about to throw away an opportunity to enjoy her company. "If you're sure, let's proceed to the library."

Stepping back into the house with him, Miss Lucci said, "I meant to ask you, what made you want to become an engineer? It seems such an unexpected choice. I understand your father is an investment banker. Wouldn't he have wanted his eldest son to join him in his business."

It was gratifying to think she was taking a personal interest in him and his work, and Kingsley walked a little taller as his chest puffed with pride. "Nothing would please Father more, but he also fully supports my interests in engineering. When I was about nine years old, I wandered into the basement of our New York home and was fascinated by all the mechanical equipment needed to heat our house and send water through the pipes. I must have asked our maintenance man a million questions, until he finally sent me on my way. Since then, I've always enjoyed seeing how things work, and looking for ways to make them work better. I can't imagine I'd be happy trying to understand stocks and bonds, and loans. I'd much rather look at the inner workings of a boiler, or take apart a washing machine and put it back together again. Believe it or not, plumbing and pipes actually interest me."

Miss Lucci laughed and Kingsley was sure it was the most musical sound he had ever heard.

Encouraged, he continued on. "I graduated near the top of my class, but that didn't ensure the job offers would come pouring in. In the world of engineering, one is required to prove one's worth. If I had chosen to be an investment banker, like my father, the doors would have been opened wide, but that isn't how I want to make my mark in this world. I prefer to work for my living by building things, and not merely sit behind a desk to count other people's money."

While his social peers had been busy taking classes in corporate law, Kingsley had set his sights on building bridges and designing projects that would stand the test of time. Granted, he may have met Mr. Branson at the Slone's house party, but Kingsley believed it was his knowledge of structural engineering that had most impressed the master architect. It was Mr. Branson's renowned talent that had enabled him to become rich, and not merely his numerous commissions from his cache of elite and wealthy clients.

"I'm quite impressed, Signore Kingsley. So plumbing and pipes hold your interest?"

"Along with bridges and dams. I guess anything that has to do with water and waterworks interests me. Funny, I hadn't quite thought of it that way before."

"I shouldn't be surprised. Your family's home has a commanding view of the Hudson River. I would think this had some influence on you."

They had reached the library, and Kingsley automatically reached to close the wide pocket doors that would shut them off from the rest of the house as he normally did when working.

Miss Lucci eyed his actions. "I thought we had agreed to leave the doors opened," she said, speaking in Italian.

"Oh, yes. Habit, I suppose." Even though he didn't like it, Kingsley pushed back the doors to their open position. The lack of privacy had him feeling as if they were being put on display for anyone who happened by, even though all of his family knew he was working with Miss Lucci on this project. He was probably being irrational and tried to set it out of his mind. After all, he hadn't been alone with a woman outside his family since he had stopped seeing Consuelo.

His ego had taken a beating after being rejected by Mrs. Vanderbilt when he had proposed marriage to her daughter, but Kingsley still believed in himself. Consuelo had loved him, that wasn't the issue. The problem was with Mrs. Vanderbilt and the damnable ways society had of placing a value on everything and everyone. They were perfectly happy to have a house full of boring old art work that no one appreciated, as long as the pieces were known to be costly and valuable. To consider anything so trite as aesthetics or good design seemed beyond them.

Thankfully, there was no need to reveal something so demeaning as his past rejection to Miss Lucci. Certainly, there were plenty of people who knew what happened, Mrs. Vanderbilt had made certain of that, but since Miss Lucci didn't run in those same circles of society, he had very little reason to believe she would ever hear about how he'd been so harshly rebuffed by Consuelo's mother. And even if she did, it was old news. He refused to let it bother him anymore. Still, it didn't escape his notice that Miss Lucci didn't have a family here in New York who could reject him as Mrs. Vanderbilt had once done.

Kingsley pulled out the chair for Miss Lucci as she took her seat at the library work table. "See, everything is exactly as we left it. Shall we pick up where we left off?" he asked.

"Unless you wish to review what we went over yesterday?" Hands clasped in front of her on the table, Miss Lucci looked very much like a prim and proper schoolteacher.

"Not necessary. I think we can proceed from here. I'd like to make as much progress as we can in what little time we have." Kingsley took his chair next to hers.

"A sound idea. Let's begin. When you're ready, you can start reading. In the original Italian first and then converted to English." Sounding very much like a dedicated tutor, it seemed Miss Lucci was intent on maintaining a strict student/teacher relationship with Kingsley.

That didn't bother him. He had a feeling, if they spent enough time together, she would eventually see him as more than just another one of the Goddards who needed help speaking her language. Eventually, he hoped she would not only see him as a man interested in pipes and plumbing, but as a man deeply interested in her affections.

They spent the next hour together immersed in the melodious sounds of Italian. At one point, Kingsley asked Miss Lucci if she would read through a section, claiming he wanted to develop a better ear for the correct pronunciation. Her accent and the way she spoke were such music to his ears, and he wished he could listen to her all night long, certain he would never grow weary of her voice.

When their time together was over, she once again headed off on her own, and Kingsley went to prepare for dinner. It seemed a shame she wasn't allowed to put on a pretty gown and join him for dinner, but regardless of how he felt about Miss Lucci, he doubted Mother would ever allow any of her staff to sit at her table.

CHAPTER 6

Kingsley's brother Jayson arrived late Saturday evening looking disgruntled and disheveled from his travels. He had missed dinner, which sorely disappointed their mother, and soon after greeting the family, went straight to the billiard room to look for a bottle of brandy. In the past, Jayson would have stayed in the parlor with Mother, entertaining her with stories from his friends at school, but this time it seemed he had no patience for such congenial conversation. Kingsley followed him into the male sanctuary, but didn't join his brother as he poured himself a drink.

"Was the trip out here really all that bad?" Kingsley asked, taking a seat on one of the plush leather armchairs near the hearth. He doubted he had ever seen his brother look quite this unkempt.

"I just finished my final exams, but at least I'm done with those damn classes at university. Father made it clear this was to be my last year and I was so far behind, I had to work doubly hard to get through the work. Most of my friends have half my work load."

"I thought most of your friends graduated last year." Like everything else he did, Jayson had been so lax in his course work for his first years at university, he had needed additional time to finish, taking five years to do what should have been done in four.

"Several of us stayed the extra year. I'm not the only one. Still, I've hardly had time to play. I've had to fit in three days of celebrating since

I left Harvard yesterday. You should see Franklyn Wells, he fared much worse than I." Laughing, Jayson finished off his first drink and poured more into his glass.

"Was it really all that bad?" Kingsley had always enjoyed his time at university, but it was well established he was the studious one while Jayson was the fun-loving, lady's man of the family. In some ways, he imagined his younger brother was much like their father must have been in his younger days when he was still a front office clerk at Grandfather's bank, and meeting actresses like their mother for late night dinners after the theaters closed.

"I barely made it through the year. The only reason I agreed to come home for the summer is because Father threatened to cut off my expense money if I didn't. Otherwise, I'd be in Newport or Long Island with one of my pals."

"He has tolerated a lot from you, I don't think a few weeks of playing nicely with Howard and the girls is all that bad."

Jayson shot him a look that let Kingsley know he sorely disagreed. "I'm here, aren't I? That should count for something. Don't tell me they still have you tied here for the summer. I thought you were working for that construction company in New York."

"Architectural firm. Branson and Millard," Kingsley corrected him.

"Construction, architecture, whatever, my point is weren't you working in New York?"

"I'm here working on some research for a project we're bidding on in Newport. Maybe you've heard, Bailey's Beach Resort is thinking of improving and expanding their private beach."

"That pile of rocks. It's amazing it's as popular as it is. As much as I love the parties of Newport, I hate that beach. Walking on it is like having my feet beaten to death. So, what kind of research?"

Kingsley was fairly certain Jayson's question was only for conversation, not because he really cared, but Kingsley couldn't help but take advantage of the opportunity to discuss his current project. He told Jayson about the design for the saltwater swimming pools he was working on and how he was translating an original reference book on the subject of Roman baths with the help of the Italian governess, Miss Lucci.

"So, you're back in the classroom with the rest of our siblings," Jayson mocked. "Why am I not surprised? Studious Kingsley, ever with your nose in a book. Children should be allowed to play when the weather is warm, not cooped up in some upstairs nursery learning another language they'll hardly ever use."

"I always enjoyed our time here in the summer." Even if he did spend most mornings tucked up in the upstairs classroom, it had still left him with the whole afternoon to play. He had used much of the classroom time to read about the wonders of the newly emerging industrial age of machines and the marvelous devices being invented. "Besides, Miss Lucci is teaching them plays while they learn Italian. It's not that bad. You'll get to see them perform their latest play tomorrow."

"So I've heard. I can hardly wait." The tone of his voice indicated otherwise. "You were already, what, fourteen, fifteen by the time Mother and Father had this place built. You were used to traveling all over Europe with those awful German nursemaids. When we finally got a decent summer home like the rest of my friends, I had hoped we would spend our time here rowing, and swimming, and fishing, not taking more lessons before we were allowed to go out and play. Then, before I knew what hit me, they had me shipped off to university."

Poor little Jayson! He had always been small for his age, and because his birthday was late in the year he had consistently argued he should be allowed extra time to catch up, giving him an extra year in the home classroom, an extra year at prep-school, and an extra year before he started university, waiting until he was nearly nineteen. As if all that weren't enough, he had taken five years to complete his university studies. Kingsley had very little compassion for his younger brother's work ethic, even if he did admire how easy Jayson made life look.

"Yes, and you spent the first two years barely making it through the minimum classes to stay enrolled."

"As long as Father's paying, I'm playing." Jayson took another sip of his drink. At least the speed of his consumption had slowed. "So, what time are we expected for this command performance by Howard and the girls?"

"After we've been to church services and lunch."

"I may be there for lunch, but don't look for me at church. I'll be sleeping in."

"I'll be sure to pass your regrets along to Mother when I see her at breakfast." Kingsley stood, ready to call it a night. There would be plenty of time to hear his brother continue his rantings the next day. "Goodnight, Jayson."

"Goodnight, grumpy old brother." Jayson raised his nearly empty glass in a parting salute.

Shaking his head in silent disapproval, Kingsley exited the room and headed upstairs. Grumpy old brother indeed. At least he had his research work with Miss Lucci to keep him happily occupied. Jayson, no doubt, would soon be going out of his head with boredom.

As Kingsley prepared for bed, his thoughts continued to center on Miss Lucci. It was bad enough that his mind, and body, insisted on drawing up images of her, but knowing she slept in the same house not so very far away only served to further his frustration.

Although he had never been up in the servants' quarters—he'd never had a reason to go there—he could still imagine her asleep in her bed. In households such as this, it was an unspoken rule that unless there was a problem, the family pretty much stayed away from where the servants slept out of respect for their privacy. If any member of a wealthy family—male or female—were to venture into the servants' quarters, it would most likely be for the sole purpose of seeking out one of the downstairs staff for some illicit sexual encounter. Not that he was against such affairs. He wasn't exactly a monk himself. But he respected Miss Lucci much too much to ever consider putting her in such an improper predicament.

It would probably hit him hard to see the small room assigned to Miss Lucci filled with her personal belongings. And the last thing he needed was to picture her dressed for bed in some sweet, little nightgown, as close to naked as a woman could be without actually . . .

It was best for him to halt this fantasy if he had any hope of getting some sleep. Still, he couldn't help but take his desires in hand long enough to achieve at least some measure of relief.

~*~

Shortly after lunch on Sunday, Kingsley, Jayson, and his parents made their way to the music room to see his younger siblings perform their play, The Shoemaker and The Elves. The music room did duty as their makeshift theater with the forward part of the room set up as the stage. Facing the stage, a row of chairs was arranged for the attending audience, the rest of the family members. Setting the scene for the play were a couple of chairs and a work table that served as the shoemaker's workshop. An ornamental screen was placed off to one side to shield the ones who were not on stage for any given scene.

Howard, being the only boy in the group, was not only given the most lines to say, he was also allowed to introduce the play and his fellow actors to their audience. Kingsley joined his mother and father in beaming their smiling support for the younger Goddards' performances.

Jayson simply looked bored.

Not surprising, since Kingsley suspected Jayson couldn't understand what was being said. What bothered him even more were the overly appreciative glances Jayson repeatedly leveled at Miss Lucci. At one point, Kingsley was sorely tempted to tell his brother to knock it off, but out of respect to Miss Lucci and the rest of his siblings, he remained quiet. Watching his brother make a fool of himself was bad enough; he didn't want to risk causing an unpleasant scene that would disrupt his younger siblings' performance. Doing his best to ignore his brother, Kingsley focused his attention back on the play, which was delightfully entertaining, and more than once, he silently gave credit for the wonderful results to Miss Lucci.

Dina and Sandra were particularly cute dressed in wings with wispy layers of gauzy silk. Playing the two shoemaking elves, they flawlessly repeated their lines in unison following Helen's lead. It appeared Vivien took her role as the shoemaker's wife quite seriously. Either that, or her nerves were getting the best of her. She didn't crack a smile through her

71

whole performance. Perhaps it was her way of portraying a sad, poor, old woman.

At the end of the play, after Howard and his sisters had taken their bows, they once again gathered at the front of the room. "We have one last piece to perform," Howard said, still speaking in Italian. "For our closing piece, we're pleased to sing a song I've written with the help of Vivien, Helen, and Miss Lucci called the Shoemaker and His Elves." Looking proud enough to burst, he beamed an appreciative, if somewhat nervous smile at his sisters and governess before taking a seat at the piano. Howard was the one with musical talent in their family. If anyone were destined to make his mark in the world of entertainment, it would be him.

Miss Lucci smiled politely back, no doubt extremely pleased with her star student.

Kingsley was sitting closest to where Miss Lucci was standing, and when she began to sing along with his siblings, her voice, so beautifully melodious, was the only one he heard. He could listen to her sing for hours and not grow weary. If only there were a way to capture her voice and have it available to be heard again and again. Perhaps it was an idea worth some thought, if only he were more of an inventor, and not simply a mechanical innovator.

When the song was over, Kingsley stood and clapped along with his mother and father. As always, Mother clapped the loudest, shouting "Bravo, bravo!" She spread her arms wide and rushed to embrace her children in one large hug. Dina and Sandra nestled in first for her show of affection, followed soon after by Vivien and Helen. "You were all marvelous, simply marvelous." When she had finished with the girls, Mother reached out to pull Howard forward. "Come now, don't be shy. You're not too old to give your mother a hug. Your performance was magnificent."

"Magnificent, now that it's finally over," Jayson grumbled as he slowly stood.

"Did we interrupt your nap time?" Several times during the play, Kingsley had noticed his brother's eyes were closed. If it hadn't been for the high-backed chairs, Jayson's head would have been bobbing on his chest.

"Is there something wrong, dear?" Mother released Howard and hovered over Jayson, laying her hand upon his forehead. That was so like her. She would rather pretend Jayson was ill than admit he simply wasn't paying attention to the rest of his family.

"Nothing some fresh air and a good ride won't fix," Father said, giving Jayson a firm look of disapproval. "Why don't you join me at the stables and we'll take a ride out to Trapper's Hill?"

It wasn't an invitation Jayson was allowed to turn down. Father obviously wanted to speak to his second son alone and if Jayson knew what was good for him, he'd accept.

Unfortunately, Jayson rarely seemed to know what was good for him. Either that, or he simply didn't care enough to try. Kingsley really did feel sorry for Jayson, in a brotherly sort of way. Besides being innately lazy, Jayson had a habit of making life harder on himself than necessary. If he spent as much energy trying to comply with Father's wishes as he did fighting them, he would have a much easier time of it.

"Am I allowed time to change first, or do you want me to go riding in my morning suit?" Jayson responded in a tone Kingsley never would have used with their father. But then again, Kingsley respected Father in a way that seemed beyond Jayson's abilities.

"By all means, go change. But I expect to see you at the stables in fifteen minutes. Don't make me wait." Father glared pointedly at Jayson before following Mother out of the room as she steered the rest of the children toward the breakfast room for refreshments.

Kingsley hung back to speak with Miss Lucci while she straightened up the room after the performance. "Now that the play is done, I expect you have the rest of the day free for yourself," Kingsley said as she gathered up the props used in the play.

"There's always more to do." Miss Lucci stacked some old shoes in a carrying basket along with the other items she had collected. Next, she turned to gather the music sheets from the piano.

"I didn't know you sang so well. You were wonderful." Kingsley picked up the basket full of props and followed Miss Lucci to the piano.

"Please, just set that basket here," she said, pointing to the piano bench. "I'll have one of the other nursery maids help me with it later. I'm glad you enjoyed the performance. The children did a great job, wouldn't you agree?"

Kingsley set the basket down as she had asked. "Howard and the girls were great, but I'm sure it's because they have such a wonderful teacher."

Miss Lucci paused in what she was doing. "I thank you for the accolade, Signore Kingsley, but I'm only doing my job. It's the children who deserve your praise."

Was that how she felt about him, and their time together? That she was only doing her job? He certainly hoped not, but as he thought about it, she really hadn't given him any reason to think anything else. Other than the fact that he found her beautiful, charming, intelligent, and with a voice like a songbird. But it seemed she thought of him as no more than another obligation, one of her many chores in the Goddard household.

Still, it didn't seem too much to ask for her to show some sign of enthusiasm for their work together. "So, will I see you again tomorrow? For our regular session."

Miss Lucci smiled brightly. "Of course, Signore Kingsley. At five o'clock for our appointed hour. I look forward to our lesson."

He didn't like to think of them as lessons, or of Miss Lucci as his tutor. He preferred to think of her as a collaborating partner. Nonetheless, her beaming smile gave him hope. "Until tomorrow then." Sensing it would become awkward if he continued to linger, Kingsley turned and exited the room.

He was barely halfway down the hall when he heard Jayson call out to him. "Aren't you a little old to be vying for the honor of teacher's pet?"

His brother had been spying on him.

"I'm working with Miss Lucci on the translation of one of my reference books on Roman baths. I simply wanted to confirm our next appointment." Kingsley kept walking but Jayson hurried to stay right on his heels. It galled him to know his brother had noticed his attentions to Miss Lucci. Knowing Jayson, he would think of some way to make his association with her seem inappropriate.

"Hmm, you know, I could use some help with my Italian. Do you think she'd be up for giving me private lessons? Late at night, in my room? Imagine the words she could teach me."

Kingsley halted in midstride, his hands fisted at his sides. "Stay away from her, Jayson. She's not one of the kitchen maids you use for your amusement." More than one pretty young maid had been forced to leave their employment because Jayson couldn't keep his hands off the hired help. His younger brother often acted as if he had the right to bed a girl simply because she worked in the kitchen. When it was discovered, as it often was, Mother or Father tried to set things right by making arrangements for the young woman to be placed in another position within their wide circle of friends. Nevertheless, Kingsley doubted such compensation completely erased the shame of being mistreated by their employer's son.

"So, you want her for yourself?" Jayson scoffed. Holding his hands in the air in a gesture of surrender, he added, "Should I feel threatened?"

"Consider yourself warned. Feel threatened if you like." Kingsley was half a foot taller than Jayson and several pounds heavier. As boys, he was consistently the victor in their backyard scuffles. Now that they were grown men, Kingsley had no desire to engage in a fistfight with Jayson. But by God, he would kick his brother's ass if Jayson so much as said an unkind word to Miss Lucci.

Turning on his heel, Kingsley strode purposefully down the hall, putting as much distance as possible between him and his offensive younger brother.

~*~

Monday evening, Kingsley nearly bounced into the library as he looked forward to his session with Miss Lucci. When she arrived, he left the pocket doors opened, as she preferred, even though he privately wished he could close them.

As they were taking their seats at their work table, Miss Lucci turned to him and said, "I appreciated your visit to the classroom this morning. I think it pleases Howard and your sisters to have their eldest brother take such an interest in them. I know it pleases me."

"It was my pleasure, Miss Lucci," Kingsley said with a smile. "I hope my presence wasn't a disruption."

"Not at all," she assured him, returning his smile. "You're welcome anytime."

Heat seeped up his spine, sparked by her words of encouragement. Earlier in the day, Kingsley had gone to the classroom to visit his younger siblings and see what they were working on with Miss Lucci. Although not surprised, he'd been peeved to find Jayson lounging on the window seat of the room, propped up by half a dozen cushions. He wasn't participating in the lesson Miss Lucci was conducting, he only seemed to be observing in a deviant sort of way.

Vivien had told him later, after lunch, that Jayson's presence seemed to make Miss Lucci nervous. She claimed Miss Lucci was noticeably relieved when Kingsley arrived and Jayson suddenly found a reason to leave, claiming Mother was expecting him.

Short of locking his brother in his room, there was damnably little Kingsley could do to keep him from bothering Miss Lucci, but he could, and would, keep an eye on him. Frustrating as it was, it seemed Jayson was intent on making a nuisance of himself.

"I love seeing how well they respond to your methods," Kingsley offered. "You have a wonderful way of making it fun to learn a foreign language. I wish my tutors growing up were half as engaging as you."

"Thank you. That's very kind of you."

It was the closest he could come to declaring his feelings for her and yet his words were little more than a well-mannered compliment. Kingsley wanted desperately to let her know how he felt, but found it hard to be so open and revealing. Jayson, undoubtedly, would know how to sprout words of affection—he did it to most every woman he met— but Kingsley found it hard to venture too far from his comfortable role of scholarly engineer. Sometimes it seemed, though only twenty-seven years old, he was only a few steps away from being a stodgy old professor. All that was missing were the wire-rimmed spectacles and an ill-fitting tweed jacket.

"Well, then, shall we proceed? I believe we were on page two-seventy-six," Miss Lucci said, getting back to business.

Kingsley realized he'd been staring, at her eyes, her lips, and the gentle curve of her cheeks, and looked away as he reached for the textbook, hastily turning to the page she mentioned. "Yes, right. The translation. I suppose we should get right to work."

Kingsley's session with Miss Lucci went exceedingly well and they made great progress working through the translation. At this pace, they could easily have the book finished in another two or three days. As satisfying as their results were, Kingsley was starting to wish there were a way to slow down their progress. He wanted to spend more time with Miss Lucci, alone. More and more, he imagined ways he might see her away from the house and all the inquisitive eyes and ears of his loving but meddlesome family. All too soon, the clock over the mantle struck six o'clock, indicating their time together was over.

Miss Lucci flinched at the sound of the clock's chime with a look of disappointment. It seemed she was as surprised as Kingsley to know their time was up.

"It seems we should stop now, since we've reached the end of this page," she said, sounding somewhat hesitant. "I'll mark our spot and we can begin here tomorrow. For now, I must excuse myself. I'm expected up in the nursery to dine with Miss Claudine and Miss Cassandra."

As much as he hated to let her go, Kingsley acquiesced. "They're lucky to have you as a dining companion. I wish I could be so lucky," he said, feeling distinct envy for his youngest sisters.

"I hardly think you want to start taking your meals in the nursery," Miss Lucci said, laughing off his comment.

She was right, of course. That hardly seemed appropriate, but something he would truly consider if it meant spending more time with her. "Maybe someday, perhaps you could join me." He knew better than to think she would be welcomed at his mother's table. "Maybe someday, when you're not busy, we could go to the village and have dinner at the Crescent Moon," he offered, referring to the best restaurant Tarrytown had to offer.

She stood abruptly. "That's very kind of you, Signore Kingsley, but I don't see how that is possible. Certainly you know, I mean, I have too many duties to be . . . well, to consider such a thing. Now, if you will excuse me, I really must go."

Before he had a chance to say anything more, she turned and hurried out of the room. *Damn.* That hadn't gone well. He hadn't expected his request to dine with Miss Lucci would create such a response. Her discomfort was so clearly evident. Perhaps he had been reading more into her kindness and friendly behavior than she intended.

Kingsley sat staring for a long moment at the open door, wishing she would return, before turning away with a shake of his head. What a fool he'd been. His only saving grace was that no one had been there to see it. Returning his attention back to the work table, he began organizing it to be ready for the next session. He was putting the pencils back into their holder when he heard someone enter the room.

"Has your little governess retreated back to her classroom upstairs? You can't honestly believe one of our servants would actually have dinner with you in town? What would the neighbors say?" It was Jayson, standing at the door to the library with a drink in his hand, mocking him.

Another reason why he should have closed those damn pocket doors. More than once during his time with Miss Lucci, he felt as if they were being watched, and suspected it was Jayson who spied on them.

"Shouldn't you be getting ready for dinner? Or are you just going to continue drinking the night away?" Kingsley shoved the last stack of their notes into his research folder and set the reference book on top of it as Jayson stepped closer.

"Does Miss Lucci know you were once rejected by the high and mighty Mrs. Vanderbilt? Or is she too much of a gold-digger to care about your past?" Jayson's tone was deliberately cruel.

Quick as a bursting water main, Kingsley stood and smacked Jayson hard in his chest. His brother stumbled backwards, landing on the back of a sofa, and spilled his drink over the front of his shirt.

Miss Lucci wouldn't care about his past any more than he cared about hers, but he wouldn't let Jayson or anyone else call her a gold-digger. Never for a moment had she shown an interest in his fortune. If anything, his wealth was a factor against him. Miss Lucci seemed to think the wealthy couldn't be trusted. With men like his brother as part of their ranks, she had good reasons for her beliefs.

"I'm warning you, Jayson. You're about two steps away from getting your ass kicked. I don't care what Mother or Father will say. I swear, if you don't back off from this, you'll be sorry."

Jayson rubbed a hand over his chest where Kingsley had struck him, as if wiping away the spilled alcohol. From the look on his face, it was obvious the blow had caused his brother considerable pain. Good for him.

"Reduced to using our fists, now, are we? How positively primitive. I thought gallant scholars were above all that."

"Back off, Jayson, or you'll see just how primitive I can be." Kingsley pushed past his brother and exited the room. A moment ago he had been in heaven enjoying the company of Miss Lucci, and now it felt as though he were in hell doing battle with the devil.

CHAPTER 7

Kingsley had planned to stay at least a few more days to take advantage of Miss Lucci's company, but on Tuesday morning he received a letter from Mr. Branson asking him to make the trip to San Francisco without delay. It seemed there was some concern regarding the viability of the project and Mr. Branson wanted Kingsley to gather firsthand information on the Sutro saltwater baths at his soonest. Before he left on the afternoon train back to New York to make arrangements for his travels west, Kingsley had a few matters he needed to settle.

Lunch had just ended and his younger siblings, with the exception of Jayson, were out on the terrace enjoying the sunny day. Howard was busy setting up a game of croquet on the lawn while Dina and Sandra stood to one side whacking a ball back and forth to each other with their brightly colored mallets. Helen was giving Howard directions on where to place the wickets, not that he needed them, and Vivien sat relaxing on a lounge chair watching them as if she were more amused than interested in playing. It gave Kingsley the opportunity he'd been looking for.

"I was thinking of walking down to the rose garden. Care to join me?" Kingsley asked Vivien as he came to stand beside her.

"And miss this game? Certainly, by all means." Standing, she reached out and hooked her hand in the bend of his arm, indicating for him to lead the way. When they had gone beyond the hearing of their siblings, she asked, "So what is it you want to talk about?"

80

"What makes you think I have something particular I want to discuss?" Kingsley feigned ignorance, although he knew his sister was smarter than that. She had made her debut two seasons ago, and from the rumors he'd heard, was soon expecting a proposal from the man of her choice. Kingsley expected Mr. Thomas Hollingsworth believed he was the one doing the pursuing, not the one being pursued.

"Please, Kingsley. You've been hanging around the classroom and our Miss Lucci since the day you got here. You can't possibly believe your attentions have gone unnoticed."

"Has Mother said anything to you?"

"No, not that she would. While she might suspect your affection for our Italian governess, I doubt she would give it much credit. She knows you're scheduled to go to San Francisco. I'm sure she expects this is nothing more than a momentary flirtation."

That was fine, for now. The less his family suspected his true feelings for Miss Lucci, the better for him. He led his sister down to the rose garden to stroll through the large open space filled with dozens of blooming flowers. For this conversation, he thought it best to avoid the higher hedges of the lover's garden where they risked being overheard by an unseen intruder, such as Jayson.

"I will confess, I've enjoyed working with Miss Lucci, but only to you because I know you can keep a secret." Of all his siblings, he was closest to Vivien, even though he was seven years her senior. When she was born, he had taken it upon himself to become her protector and they had remained close as she matured. He rather liked being the big brother she could count on to lend a sympathetic shoulder when she needed a good cry or when they conspired together against their other siblings.

"And you'd keep mine. So, what is it you need?"

"While I'm gone, I'd like you to keep an eye on Miss Lucci, especially where Jayson is concerned. He's made some disparaging remarks about her, and I don't trust him. I believe he would make a play for her just to spite me, not because he cares. I don't want to see her abused by him."

"Nor would I. Miss Lucci is too kindhearted for Jayson. You have my word. I'll keep an eye on things." Vivien leaned over to smell one of the blood red roses blooming on the bush beside her. "It's sad to see Jayson so . . . I don't know, so despondent. Especially since he's come home from university."

"Jayson has had the same opportunities as you and I. He simply chooses to disregard his benefits. Instead, he acts as if life is out to get him." It galled him the way Jayson wasted his life. Though the Goddards had enough wealth to support Jayson's indolent lifestyle twice over, that didn't mean he should squander his resources. "I worry for him too, but until Jayson wants to change, he won't."

Vivien let out a heavy sigh. "Yes, I know. Mother and Father have both tried."

"Mother coddles him too much."

"She has since birth. It's too late to change now."

Much of the reason for the four and a half years' age difference between Kingsley and Jayson was due to their mother having suffered a stillbirth the year after Kingsley was born. The loss of her first daughter was devastating to Edith Goddard, and it took her several months to recover. When she became pregnant again, she worried so much about losing another baby, she was nearly overwhelmed with both joy when Jayson was born, and a never-ending concern for his well-being. Jayson was always a little small for his age, and though he wasn't the daughter she had hoped for, she had denied him nothing until he developed a righteous sense of entitlement that seemed impossible to dislodge. Kingsley grew up believing he needed to take care of himself, whereas Jayson grew up believing Mother would provide anything he wanted. Sadly, Father did nothing to dissuade Mother or Jayson of this idea until it was too late to fix the damage that had already been done.

"Wise beyond your years. I've always liked that about you." Kingsley said.

"Just how serious are your intentions toward Miss Lucci?" Vivien looked up at him with imploring eyes. If it was anyone else, he would have ducked the question, but it felt good to have someone he could confide in.

"It's too soon to tell. I think she likes me, but there are times when it seems I'm only another one of her students, like you, and Howard, and the girls."

"I highly doubt that. I've seen you two together. She's far more interested than you may think."

"You wouldn't say that just to get my hopes up, would you?" He could think of a dozen different reasons why attempting a relationship with Miss Lucci was a bad idea, but none of that seemed to matter. The only thing that mattered was how much he liked her, and how his insides tangled up in knots whenever she was near.

"Never." Vivien gave him a knowing smile that lit her young face. Some man out there was in for big trouble.

"What am I to do? I must leave this afternoon to catch the train back to New York. Mr. Branson wants me out in San Francisco by the end of the week." Kingsley sat heavily on a nearby bench and looked back toward the house. Miss Lucci was up there somewhere, no doubt preparing for her next class with his siblings. He hadn't yet told her of his imminent departure.

"Well, let me think." Vivien took a seat beside him. "If it was me, and the man of my dreams was about to be gone for an extended trip, at the very least, I'd want to know I could expect to see him again, and that he would miss me while he was gone."

"I highly doubt I'm the man of her dreams." Kingsley tried to laugh but the sound was more of a grunt.

"Men, so slow to learn. To *be* the man of her dreams, you must first act as if you are. No woman wants a lukewarm suitor. Let her know there's some fire behind those eyes. Take your nose out of those books and let her see a bit of the real you."

Kingsley had been a scholar all his life, and a methodical thinker. He liked to know how things worked. He was famous for taking things apart, and trying to make them better as he put them back together.

Vivien was suggesting he take action without a care for the consequences.

"You've always been my knight in shining armor," Vivien said, patting his arm with affection. "But Miss Lucci has only known you for a few days. Don't you think a show of confidence and daring will make a good impression?"

"A show of daring? What exactly would you suggest?"

"Let her know you'll miss her while you're gone."

He hadn't even left and he already missed her. She was there in his daydreams, and joined him each night in his dreams as he slept. "I worry she'll think I'm too forward, or too aggressive, using my position over her to her disadvantage."

Vivien nodded knowingly. "I understand your concern. The master's son mixing with the hired help rarely has a good outcome for the servant."

"I don't think of her as a servant."

"Maybe you don't, but everyone else does, especially her."

"Then you see my problem." Leaning forward, Kingsley rested his arms on his knees and shook his head, disappointed and frustrated.

From the moment they met, he saw Miss Lucci as an intelligent, charming, and beautiful woman. She seemed perfectly capable of taking care of herself. After all, she had managed to leave her home in Italy without the aid of a man and find suitable work for a woman of her talents that was respectable and rewarding. There was a lot to admire about her.

"But what are your options? If you leave here without making your feelings known, she'll think she means nothing to you, and will undoubtedly return the sentiment. If you let her know how you feel, and she rejects you, which I highly doubt, as least you'll know where you stand. And since you have to leave anyway, the repercussions will be short-lived."

Maybe for her, but not for him. "Seems a risk, either way."

"Come now, Kingsley. You design bridges and stuff," she said, fluffing her hand through the air. "There's an element of risk in everything we do. Take a chance. Build yourself a bridge."

Damn, his sister was right. Although he didn't really design bridges, mostly he designed conveyance systems to move water from one place to another. But still, he understood her meaning. Women were definitely the smarter of the species. Poor Mr. Hollingsworth didn't have a chance. If she had truly set her sights on him, as Kingsley suspected, the man was as good as married.

~*~

Kingsley strode decisively through the house looking for Miss Lucci. To his great relief, he found her alone in the library sitting near one of the large floor-to-ceiling windows reading a book. She looked up as he came in.

"Miss Lucci, I'm so glad I found you." Catching his breath, Kingsley closed the pocket door behind him.

"Signore Kingsley. Is everything alright?" she asked, setting aside her book.

"I had to see you. I've come to say goodbye. I'm being sent to San Francisco, for my project. I'll be leaving for New York soon to make the necessary arrangements."

"Oh! So, I guess we won't be meeting this afternoon for our time together."

He liked that she didn't call it a lesson, or even a session. She called it their *time* together. "I didn't want to leave without saying goodbye." He took a step forward and she stood to meet him.

"That's very, umm . . . considerate of you." She looked up at him with her soft, doe-like eyes and his heart melted like a piece of chocolate held too tightly in one's fist.

He took another step closer. "I wanted to let you know, I'll be back. In a few weeks. No more than a month. I'm hoping I can see you again, when I return . . . to continue the translation."

"Of course, if you still need my assistance."

"I'm sure of it. Your translation skills have proved most helpful." How lame. This was exactly what his sister had warned him against. He needed to let her know he cared, and that he thought of her as more than merely Mother's hired Italian governess, or an assistant helping him with his work.

An awkward moment of silence passed, and Kingsley suddenly blurted out, "I was hoping I could get a kiss goodbye." When her expression turned to one of shock, he added, "For good luck, of course." He couldn't believe he had said that out loud; it sounded like something Jayson would say. Holding his breath, her waited for her to answer.

"It hardly seems proper," she countered.

Kingsley let out his breath. She hadn't exactly said no, and she hadn't slapped his face, or walked away. All good signs he hadn't completely destroyed the moment, and there was still a chance he could get the kiss he wanted. "Even in the interest of good luck?" he asked taking a step closer.

Anna Maria looked slightly confused, as if considering her options. "It seems wrong to deny you good luck."

Taking another step closer, Kingsley asked, "Have you any idea how many times I've imagined kissing you?"

Her eyes grew wide, and her sweet, sensual mouth formed a round little O, making her even more tempting, more desirable. Her natural innocence was both beguiling and challenging. Without even trying, she set his heart racing. His breath caught in his chest. Everything deep inside him went tight and hard with desire. *Control yourself*, he thought. *She's a governess, for Christ's sake, translating Italian with me, not some courtesan in need of seducing.*

Ignoring his own internal warning system, he leaned in and whispered in her ear. "I've often imagined kissing you here, on your swan like neck." His hand came up to brush the slender curve of her neck. Moving his hand, his thumb padded across her cheek, "Or here." And then, touching a finger to her sweetly curved lips, he added, "or here?"

Anna Maria's eyes locked onto his, and as if by the sheer power of his will, she seemed frozen in place. Lowering her lashes, she leaned in, narrowing the gap between them. All he needed to do was pull her into his arms. Going slow to test her resistance, he tilted his head and reached for her, covering her luscious lips with his mouth. Oh, the sweet taste of her: spicy and exotic, and slightly forbidden. Warm and inviting, her lips parted ever so slightly and he felt the tip of her tongue brush lightly against his mouth. Encouraged, he pressed harder, with greater passion. Melting against him, her hands came up and cupped his head, grabbing tufts of his hair.

A second later, she pushed him away, and took a quick step back, breaking the spell. "I thought it was only a kiss for luck you wanted. This leads me to think you want something more."

Her reaction stunned him. If he weren't mistaken, she had freely participated in their kiss. Hadn't she felt anything? Surely, he wasn't the only one who sensed their connection. "Would it be so wrong if I do?"

Sadness filled her eyes, followed by anger. "Just because I'm a servant in your mother's house does not mean you can take advantage of me."

Her dizzying display of emotions left Kingsley reeling. "Miss Lucci, I swear, I meant no offense. I thought . . ."

"You thought I should *want* to kiss you, after all, I'm merely a governess, a servant in your home. But I can assure you, Signore Kingsley, I come from a good Italian family. I have been taught better than to submit to the will of a man who thinks he can have his way with me. Just because I work for my living does not mean you can do anything you please."

"Miss Lucci, I can assure you, I would never *think* such a thing." It struck him hard to hear her refer to herself as a servant. He certainly didn't see her as one.

"I find that hard to believe." Lifting her chin, she added, "It's time for me to return to the classroom. I have work to do." With a rustle of skirts, she turned and fled the room, leaving Kingsley to wonder how he could have been such an ass.

Everything had led him to believe she felt something for him. Maybe not as strongly as he felt about her, but this reaction was not at all what he had expected.

A servant! She thought he wanted to take advantage of her because she was a servant in his mother's house? How could she even think that about him? He respected her, thought of her as a collaborator and that they worked well together. Never once had he thought she was someone he could take advantage of. Did she really think so little of him, or was she simply lumping him in with the rest of high-society's wealthy class? Those who cared little if they abused the hired help?

It cut him to the bone to think she had so little trust in him. He had misjudged her, and now, once again, he paid the price with embarrassment and rejection.

When it came to women, it seemed he knew nothing at all. It was best to stick with boilers, pumps, and pipes. At least he knew how they worked, and how to fix them when they didn't.

CHAPTER 8

It took everything she had to make it through the rest of the day without giving into a fit of mental flagellation over the way she had rejected Kingsley. His kiss had taken her by surprise, and as much as she tried to resist her feelings, she couldn't deny she had enjoyed the moment more than a proper woman should.

Having completed her duties for the day, Anna Maria made her way to her room to prepare for bed. While her room was on the same floor as the nursery, it left much to be desired in the way of amenities, and she rarely spent time there other than sleeping. Thankfully, the Goddard summer home was so large, she could usually find an unoccupied room where she could hide away to read or work on one of her many embroidery projects, such as the eyeglass case she planned to send home to her mother for Christmas.

The gaslights in the servants' quarters of the house were notoriously unreliable and the single wall sconce in her room made it hard to read in the fading evening light. To provide additional light, and give her room a feeling of comfortable warmth, Anna lighted a candle next to her bed. Like a memory from home, the soft, golden, flickering glow felt soothing and filled her room with the calming scent of beeswax.

Though she tried to direct her attention to the book in her hands, her mind continued to return to Kingsley and their kiss when he came to say goodbye. His boldness had taken her by surprise, and at first, she had

89

offered no resistance. Instead, she had melted against him and flung her arms around his brawny shoulders like a shameless strumpet, letting him take the kiss deeper, delighting in its passion. It seemed Signore Kingsley was much better at kissing than she had expected. With so little experience, she hadn't known what to expect, but it certainly wasn't the desire she'd felt strumming through her body. Somehow, he had made her want to drop her defenses and lose her inhibitions.

Her first reaction had been one of unrestrained lust, followed quickly by righteous self-preservation. How dare the son of her employer think he could have his way with her? No gentleman of the upper class could ever be trusted to act honorably toward a servant.

It wasn't until much later, long after he had left the house, that she began to reevaluate what had happened. He had only asked for a kiss goodbye—for good luck he'd said—but she had reacted as if he had forced himself upon her, which certainly was not the case.

Although raised a strict and moral Catholic, she couldn't deny the tempting appeal of her employer's eldest son. Kingsley was kind, considerate, and most of all, she appreciated his thoughtful intelligence. Not that he necessarily felt the same way about her, but it was tempting to imagine that maybe he could. She also knew it was wrong to covet that which she could not have, but thoughts of desire refused to leave her head.

Closing her eyes in regret, Anna recalled how badly she had handled his attempt to bid her goodbye, and felt the sting of her foolish behavior. Kingsley had sought her out in the library to say goodbye and had asked for a kiss for luck.

One sweet, wonderful, thrilling, passionate kiss.

And even though she had enjoyed it immensely, she had fled from the scene as if the wolves of hell were at her heels. What a ninny.

Never once had Kingsley indicated he intended to take advantage of her, and yet her natural mistrust of anyone with wealth and position had kicked in and she had thought the worst. She had even been so boldly stupid as to suggest he was trying to take advantage of her. After her show of sanctimonious prudishness, it was highly unlikely he would ever want to work with her again, much less seek out her company. And now that he was gone, there was no way to let him know how she felt, or try to make amends.

Perhaps that was for the best. It seemed the longer she spent in his company, the closer she came to letting down her guard, and if she hoped to continue working as a governess for the social elite, the one thing she couldn't risk was her reputation.

Too distracted to read, Anna Maria tossed aside her book, setting it down on her dresser harder than she intended. In the process, she knocked over the candle, spilling wax across the polished wood surface.

"*Mannaggia!*" Anna cursed in her native tongue. "Now look what I've done." Grabbing her face cloth from the wash basin, she hurried to wipe up the mess but only proceeded to make it worse, spreading the melted wax as she wiped. What she needed to do was wait for it to cool and harden so she could easily scrape it off with a butter knife and a polishing rag. In her haste, she had ruined the face cloth and had done more damage than good to the dresser.

Disgusted with herself, she tossed the ruined washcloth into the wastebasket.

Difficult as it was to admit, Anna realized she needed to let go of her preconceived expectations and judgments of Kingsley. Just because he came from a wealthy family didn't mean he intended to take advantage of her, as the Dovers had done. But their lack of consideration for her feelings and opinions had left a hurtful bruise on her ego. Adding to her feelings of doubt and mistrust were the actions of Mr. Jayson. Since his return to the Goddards' summer home, she had repeatedly caught Mr. Jayson leering at her as if she were a savory cut of meat, and his comments were often laced with upsetting innuendo about providing him with private lessons and letting him show her what a good student he could be. It left her feeling exposed and vulnerable.

While none of that excused her dismissive behavior toward Kingsley, it helped explain why she had rejected him, lumping him in with his younger brother and all the rest of his class as being against her.

Though she knew Kingsley was not like the rest, when confronted with his passionate desires, she had mistrusted herself and made untrue assumptions. It was like that book she had read while living in London by Miss Jane Austen, *Pride and Prejudice*, where Miss Bennet's pride allows her to misjudge Mr. Darcy. Much like Miss Bennet, Anna had allowed her prejudice to cloud her opinion of Signore Kingsley. He was nothing but kind and considerate toward her and everyone he met, but because of his wealth and education she had discounted his intentions as being superficial. In reality, she was the superficial one, with her persistent disdain for his class of society.

Kingsley didn't deserve her harsh rebuff, but at the time, her reaction had been purely instinctive. She had reacted out of fear, and panic, and self-preservation. Partly, it was because she found it hard to believe he really cared for her. But mostly, she was too afraid of being taken advantage of and made to look like a fool. Or of being discarded and handed off to another as Mrs. Dover had done when she handed her off to Mrs. Goddard.

Ironically, if none of that had happened, if Mrs. Dover hadn't handed her off to Mrs. Goddard, Anna would have never met Signore Kingsley. And never would have experienced the pleasure of his company, or the passion of his kiss.

Since Kingsley's departure for New York, even though the big house was full of people, it felt unreasonably empty. He was on his way to California and she had no idea if she would ever see him again.

CHAPTER 9

A nna Maria returned to the classroom early the next day ready to do her job. She may have acted horribly with Kingsley, but she was determined to not let it affect her work. Howard and the girls were planning to start work on their new play and she wouldn't let them down. For their next performance, she chose a one-act play that centered on an elaborate but amusing dinner party with a missing pet cat and a nervous maid attempting to find the fugitive feline before it had a chance to ruin the meal. Miss Helen would be perfect for the part of the maid.

One of the reasons she chose this particular play was for the many new words her students would learn. She also hoped they would enjoy its humor. Much of her free time from yesterday evening—time she would have been working with Kingsley—had been dedicated to writing out copies of the play to hand out to each of the children, but Anna believed it was worth her time and effort to provide them with appropriate study materials.

Anticipating a busy day, Anna was sitting at her desk, awaiting the arrival of her students when Miss Vivien entered the room alone. Being the oldest of her students, Vivien was closest to her age, younger than she by only two years. Sometimes it amazed Anna Maria to think she was only twenty-two and living on her own in America, far from her family. Yet at other times it struck her that most women her age already had husbands and homes of their own. Nonetheless, this was the life she had chosen, and she didn't believe in looking back with regrets.

Arriving before the others, Miss Vivien came and took a seat next to Anna's desk. "Howard and the girls are still down at breakfast with Mother. They're planning to take a drive along the river later today, but I wanted a few minutes to speak to you alone." Looking pretty and well dressed as always, she wore a pale yellow dress with tiny mint green leaves embroidered on the fabric. Being in her second season as a debutante, Miss Vivien spent much of her time attending various social functions in and around Tarrytown. As a result, she spent much less time in the classroom than her younger siblings, and yet Anna felt drawn to Miss Vivien's warm and welcoming personality.

"Won't you be joining them?" Anna sat with her hands clasped atop the desk in what she thought of as her governess posture.

"Not today. I plan to ride into Tarrytown to do some shopping and hoped you would accompany me as my chaperone." Miss Vivien said with a perky smile.

"Doesn't Ellie, your maid, usually act as your chaperone?" Anna asked, thinking of all the things she could do with a free afternoon.

"Yes, but she's not any fun. She's too shy and quiet. You're much more interesting and I was hoping we could spend some time together outside of the classroom. You know, Miss Lucci, just because you work in my mother's house doesn't mean we can't be friends."

Friends! No one she had worked for had ever suggested she be their friend. If there was one thing she had learned during her short tenure as a governess, it was that the upstairs family and the downstairs staff did not mingle, and that included acting as friends. "Miss Vivien, I'm your governess. I'm here to teach you Italian. I hardly think it's proper for us to be friends."

"Why? It's not like you're one of the serving maids from the local village. You're an educated, well-traveled woman. Why wouldn't I enjoy your company? Don't you like me?"

"I like you a great deal, but you're . . ." *You're my employer's daughter. I am not your equal. And never will be.*

94

"I'm nineteen years old, already in my second season. Helen is only fifteen. I need someone closer to my age. Another woman I can talk to, and please, don't suggest my mother."

"Miss Vivien, you have plenty of friends." Anna thought of all the balls, parties, and teas Miss Vivien attended. Surely the young woman had plenty of friends to choose from to accompany her on a shopping trip into the village.

"But they're not here, and you are. Don't you ever wish you had someone to talk to?"

All the time. There were times when Anna desperately felt the need for a friend, someone close she could confide in, especially when it came to her feelings for Signore Kingsley, but working as a governess made that hard to achieve. While Anna was friendly with the other servants working for the Goddards at Riverwood, she didn't feel she could truly be herself around them. Most of the other women who worked in the house were from the local village, as Miss Vivien had said, and tended to stick together, making her feel somewhat like an outsider. Other than her time in the classroom with the children, the one person she had spoken to the most was Kingsley.

But he was gone, and Miss Vivien was very kindly asking for her assistance. "If you're sure your mother won't disapprove, I'll be happy to accompany you to Tarrytown," Anna said, squaring her shoulders.

"Mother won't mind. She'll be pleased to know I have someone to keep an eye on me, and I know she trusts you. Since you've started using plays as a way of teaching us Italian, she thinks you're wonderful. And while we're in the village, if we want to gossip about someone, we can speak Italian and no one will know what we're saying."

"Miss Vivien! You should never assume someone is unable to understand you just because you're speaking a foreign language. There are far too many immigrants here in America to take such a chance. Nor would I encourage you to gossip. However, I do like the idea of finding new ways for you to practice Italian, so your suggestion does have merit." Though she had acted appalled by Miss Vivien's suggestion that they use Italian to gossip, privately, she had to admit, there were times when she had spoken English with her brother after they had returned to Italy for much the same reasons.

"Then it's agreed. You'll accompany me to Tarrytown while Mother takes Howard and the girls riding along the river."

Anna Maria almost giggled, she felt so excited to be going on an excursion with Miss Vivien, but she refrained. It was childish to giggle. But from somewhere deep inside, feelings of joy bubbled up just the same, and she felt very much like a schoolgirl discovering she had found a new friend.

"What? You're going to Tarrytown without me and Ellie?" Miss Helen said as she walked into the room followed by Mister Howard and the twins.

"I've already gotten approval from Mother, and I know you're going riding this afternoon, so you already have plans."

Miss Helen looked as if she were about to pout, but her expression turned to one of suspicion. "Is Mr. Hollingsworth in town?"

Miss Vivien looked indifferent. "How would I know? I heard he's expected to visit the Morgans at their summer home, but that has nothing to do with my plans. I want to do some shopping and show Miss Lucci around the area. She doesn't get out enough and you go into the village all the time."

"That's fine with me. I don't want to hang around while you fawn over hats and gloves. You're always buying more, as if you don't already have enough." Miss Helen gave her sister a childishly snide grin, a strong reminder of her younger age.

"Wait until you make your debut. Then we'll see how many hats you think are enough," Miss Vivien argued.

Seeing a need to divert the girls from their spat, Anna directed the children to take a copy of the new play so they could begin learning their lines. The distraction worked perfectly. Within seconds, their attentions were focused on their scripts and the new parts they needed to learn.

After flipping through the pages, Miss Vivien declared, "I think I should have the part of the maid. She had the most lines to say."

"I was hoping to play that part. You're older, you should be playing the mistress of the house." Glancing back at her playbook, Miss Helen added, "Mrs. Oglebee."

"Yes, but the maid is funnier. You can be Mrs. Oglebee," Miss Vivien countered.

"I don't want to be Mrs. Oglebee. I want to be the maid," Miss Helen wailed.

"Mrs. Oglebee is the one who saves the day by finding the cat and taking it out to the barn where it belongs," Anna Maria offered, hoping to make the role sound more appealing to the younger sibling.

"In that case, I'll take the part of Mrs. Oglebee, and you can play the maid," Miss Vivien announced before Miss Helen could respond. "It looks as if you get what you want after all."

Miss Helen looked as if she suspected she had just been outdone by her sister, but sticking to her original request, she accepted the role of the maid. In the end, it seemed Miss Vivien was a young woman accustomed to getting what she wanted.

~*~

Shortly after Anna had dismissed the children for lunch, Miss Vivien come to her side.

"If you want, I'm sure you have time to change before we go into town. I'm thinking of wearing my light blue muslin."

Anna was wearing a plain white blouse with a grey cotton skirt, her usual attire as governess. "I hadn't thought about changing." But as she looked down at her attire, she realized it would not do for a visit into town. Her outfit made her look plain and frumpy, and marked her as a servant.

"What about your plum colored dress? It goes well with your dark hair and skin."

The outfit Miss Vivien was referring to was her Sunday best and she never thought to wear it anywhere other than to church. Since she'd begun living in the mansions of her wealthy employers, Anna had developed a taste for pretty things and she never missed an opportunity to take the castoffs of her employers to remake them into something special, such as she had done with the plum colored dress given to her by Mrs. Goddard.

"I'll look in my closet and see what I can find." Anna had made it sound as though she had dozens of dresses to choose from, when in truth, other than the skirts and blouses she wore in the classroom, she had no more than a few nice dresses. But still, a shirtwaist and skirt were not proper attire for a shopping trip in the village unless one wished to be marked as one of the working class.

"I trust your judgment. I'm sure you'll find something perfect. Can you meet me in the front foyer after lunch, say in an hour?"

"Yes, I'll be there," Anna said, and watched as Miss Vivien left the room.

While she was excited about accompanying Miss Vivien to the village, Anna reminded herself she was only there to act as chaperone. She would still be on duty and would be expected to act as such. Nonetheless, when she went to her room to check her closet, she picked a russet colored silk dress she had received from Mrs. Dover soon after she arrived in New York. It was from several seasons back, and the color was bolder than what Anna usually wore, but it seemed appropriate for a ride into Tarrytown with Miss Vivien. Unlike her usual plain white shirtwaist and grey skirt, at least it wouldn't mark her as a servant.

"I'm so glad you agreed to join me," Miss Vivien said as they climbed into the open-air landaulet that would take them to the village. "I love your dress. You look stunning. You should wear that color more often."

"Thank you, Miss Vivien," Anna responded politely. "But I hardly think this would be appropriate for the classroom." She gathered her skirts about her as she climbed in to sit beside her student, feeling more pleased by Miss Vivien's compliment than she probably should.

"Please, can you simply call me Vivien? At least when we're out on our own. I know you prefer to be formal in the classroom, but for now, I'd like to think we're just two women going shopping. I really want us to be friends. Someone I can talk to."

The landaulet started off with a bit of a jerk, forcing Anna back against the thickly cushioned seat. "I'm not sure that's a good idea." Anna didn't want to risk undermining their student/teacher relationship with the younger woman, especially since she was essentially on this outing to act as Miss Vivien's chaperone.

The disappointing look on Miss Vivien's face quickly had Anna rethinking her response. It had never occurred to Anna that perhaps Miss Vivien was as much in need of a friend as she was. "Well, maybe, if it's only when we're on an outing like this, I suppose it will be alright." She was only two years older than Miss Vivien, and by fall, would probably no longer be her teacher, much less her governess. Still, it was hard to change the way she addressed her student.

"It would mean so much to me. And must I call you Miss Lucci, or may I call you Anna?"

Only her family called her Anna. "I've always preferred Anna Maria. It sounds much nicer, don't you think?"

Vivien's face lit up with a beaming smile. "Anna Maria. Thank you. This means a lot to me."

The landaulet turned off the long drive heading out from the Goddard summer home and onto the main road leading to the village. Anna took a deep breath. The scent of lilacs filled the warm summer air. "I suppose it would be nice to have someone other than the other nursery maids to talk to," Anna admitted. Especially someone educated, who had views outside of this little corner of the world. "I know you've been to Italy. What part did you like best?" As long as they were going to be friends, they might as well get to know each other.

"Venice. It's so romantic, don't you think?" Miss Vivien replied, beaming.

"I've never been there, but I've heard a lot about it. It would be lovely to go there and float through the canals, but I'd much rather visit Florence. Some of the best museums are there."

"Museums! You sound like Kingsley. Regardless of where we traveled, he would insist on going to the museums as soon as possible.

You two should travel together sometime. I'm sure you have a lot in common."

"Miss Vivien! I hardly think that's proper," Anna gasped.

"You promised to call me Vivien."

"Nevertheless, *Vivien*, your suggestion is still quite shocking." While the idea of traveling with Signore Kingsley was shockingly alluring, she would never admit to such a thing. The thought was too dangerously appealing. And so dangerously wrong.

"It wouldn't be improper if you were with the family, like when you were with the Dovers. Besides, I know Kingsley thinks highly of you. If we ever go to Italy, you should go with us. I'm sure you'd make a great tour guide."

"I acted as tour guide for the Dovers while they were in Italy. It was my favorite time with them. The children were a handful, but they were so eager to learn. One of my fondest memories was taking them on a tour through the ruins of Pompeii and telling them about the volcano. The boys were mesmerized by the story."

"I'm not surprised. Little boys like to hear about things that blow up." Vivien laughed, setting Anna at ease.

"I think even Mr. Dover liked the story."

"Men are simply little boys who think they've grown up. That's what Mother always says." They rolled down the well-used lane, past fields of green pastures on one side and a long stretch of the Hudson River on the other.

Anna Maria realized she had not spoken much to Mrs. Goddard in the past few days. As her employer, the matriarch of the home seemed to prefer to keep her distance, allowing Anna to run her classroom pretty much as she wanted. Especially after Anna had agreed to use plays as a method for teaching the children Italian. It made her wonder if Mrs. Goddard was hoping there was an actor among her children, although surely, such a profession would surely be frowned upon by her circle of friends.

"Except for Kingsley," Miss Vivien continued. "He's been old for as long as I can remember. He's always been my protector. I've looked up to him my whole life."

"He's your oldest brother. I'm sure that's to be expected." Anna wasn't quite comfortable discussing Kingsley with his sister. Her feelings regarding him were still unsettled and she didn't want to risk saying anything that might reveal how she felt, or something she might regret.

"Not necessarily. Look at Jayson. Everyone takes Kingsley seriously because he's a serious person. He would never do anything to mislead you or hurt you. He's not like Jayson. Jayson likes to drink and party with his friends. He thinks mostly of himself. It's not really his fault, Mother simply never told him no."

"I know. They're nothing alike." A familiar pang of remorse washed over Anna. She had mistakenly lumped Kingsley in with men such as Mr. Jayson, and she'd been wrong. It was more than their age that separated them. For two brothers, they couldn't be more different.

"So you agree, Kingsley is an honorable man, and quite likable."

Anna wondered why Miss Vivien was promoting Signore Kingsley so strongly, especially to her governess, but she wasn't about to let her conflicted feelings be known. The less said, the better. "I have nothing bad to say about anyone in your family. I'm grateful for this opportunity to be of service."

"Please, Anna Maria, you're more than my governess. Remember, you promised to be my friend."

Only for today, Anna thought with pragmatic recognition of the roles they were playing. *When we return to the classroom, I'll still be your governess.* As delightful and tempting as it was to consider Miss Vivien her friend, she couldn't imagine treating one of her students as a *friend*. It would undermine any authority she hoped to maintain.

They had reached the main street of the village where the stores were located and the driver came to a stop in front of Sweet Desires, a chocolate and candy shop. He climbed down from his perch and came around to assist them out of the carriage.

101

"Meet us back here in an hour," Miss Vivien informed him. Then turning to Anna Maria, she asked, "Or should we make it longer, say an hour and a half?"

"When is Mrs. Goddard expecting you home?" Anna asked, concerned that she not disappoint her employer, especially considering this was the first time she'd been given the responsibility of accompanying Miss Vivien on an outing.

Miss Vivien turned back to the driver. "An hour and a half will be fine." She checked her watch. "Let's plan to meet here at half past three."

"I'll be waiting," he assured her.

"We'll save the sweet shop for later, after we've tired ourselves out looking in all the windows. I always like to end the day with a cup of chocolate."

Anna had brought a few dollars with her, but she had hoped she wouldn't need to spend them. Frugal to his core, her father had always encouraged the family to be thrifty, and since coming to America, Anna had saved every dollar she could in case she ever needed to return to Italy, or to tide her over should she ever lose one job before she found another. Still, she didn't want to look cheap in front of Miss Vivien. "That sounds like a splendid idea."

"It'll be my treat, of course. Mother gave me more than enough money."

Anna tried not to show her sigh of relief. "Only if you're sure."

"Trust me, I have more than enough. It wouldn't be right for you to pay. I'm the one who invited you to join me. Now, I really want to show you the millinery next door. They have the most wonderful straw hat decorated with lovely tea roses I want to try on. I simply love roses, don't you?"

Vivien wrapped her gloved hand around Anna's and began leading her down the street. The familiarity of the gesture was both disquieting and strangely reassuring. Anna wasn't used to having someone she worked for, much less one of her students, treat her with such familiarity, especially outside of the classroom. But as she thought about it, she realized she rather liked Miss Vivien's show of affection. She had come to Tarrytown with her student to act as her chaperone, and yet, Miss Vivien seemed intent on treating Anna as she would any of her friends.

"I expect every woman loves roses. They're so colorful, beautiful, and fragrant." Anna freely allowed herself to be led down the street by Miss Vivien as if this were something she did every day, rather than the truly unique experience that it was.

"Exactly. I love having our house full of them. Mother buys them from a local grower when she can't get enough from our garden. She prefers to keep lots of blooms on the bushes; she says they last longer that way and it encourages people to stroll in the garden. Mother loves to show off her gardens, as I'm sure you noticed."

"I can't blame her. The gardens at Riverwood are something to be proud of. I know I've enjoyed taking several walks there." Instantly, she recalled the time she had run into Kingsley while out on one of her walks. Only later had she realized that particular section of the garden was known as the lovers' path due to its high hedges and the additional privacy they provided. Thankfully, being the perfect gentleman that he was, Kingsley had not attempted to take advantage of their secluded setting. Although, there were times she had wondered how she would feel if she were given another opportunity.

As soon as they stepped inside the hat shop, they were greeted by a sales clerk who seemed to know Miss Vivien quite well.

"Miss Goddard, how lovely to see you again. Have you come back for the rose hat you admired on your last visit?"

"That's the one. Can you bring it out for me?" As the shop girl hastened off to retrieve the desired bonnet, Miss Vivien explained to Anna, "The last time I was here, I asked them to set it aside since I had already spent most of my shopping allowance. This time, I made sure to visit this shop first. I could have bought it on credit, of course, but Helen was with me, and I didn't want her telling Mother I had overspent my allowance."

"A very sensible idea, I'm sure." Anna wondered what it must be like to have such a plentiful supply of funds for clothes and shopping.

103

As they waited for the shop girl, Miss Vivien roamed around the room, checking out the various hats on display. Anna followed close behind.

"Oh, look at this one. It perfectly matches your dress." Miss Vivien picked up a fashionable picture hat from its stand and held it up for Anna to see.

The felted hat in a lovely shade of amber was adorned with pheasant feathers and a grosgrain bow, and Anna had to agree, it would go well with her russet dress. It also cost more than she could ever afford to spend. In contrast, Anna wore a plain, dark brown hat, practical in its ability to be worn with basically every dress she owned, and slightly old-fashioned. She hadn't bought a new hat in years, and even then, it had been at a reduced price.

"It is quite nice," Anna agreed, though she couldn't imagine buying a hat simply because it matched *one* of her dresses.

"Here, try it on," Miss Vivien insisted.

Just then, the shop girl came out from the back room holding the hat Miss Vivien had requested. "Have you found another you like?" she asked.

"Yes. I want you to assist my friend in trying on this hat."

The shop girl set down the rose-covered hat on the empty stand and took the felted hat from Vivien, ready to provide her assistance.

Anna felt trapped. She didn't want Miss Vivien, or herself, to look bad in front of the shop girl. What could it hurt to try it on? She wanted to make Miss Vivien happy, so she reached up and removed her hat from her head. The shop girl took her bonnet and dismissively set it aside before placing the new one on Anna, then adjusted it to an attractive slant.

When she took a look at herself in the mirror, Anna had to admit, she liked what she saw. The hat seemed to highlight the soft brown color of her eyes and it gave her skin a warm, golden glow. Or maybe it was just the smile on her face as she admired how she looked. Either way, she felt beautiful.

"Oh, my word, it's perfect on you. You must let me buy it for you." Miss Vivien clapped her hands together with glee.

The very idea shocked her. "Oh, no, Miss Vivien. I can't allow you to do that. I must insist."

Speaking to the shop girl, Miss Vivien said, "Could you excuse us for a moment?"

"Of course." The shop girl took a few steps away toward the back of the shop.

Speaking low, Miss Vivien said, "Anna Maria, I respect your reluctance to accept my generosity, but really, what will it hurt for me buy you a hat. It's only a hat. If I don't spend my money on this, I'll only find something else to buy for myself, and Lord knows, I don't need another hat. Think of it as my way of saying thank you for coming with me and not making me get stuck with Ellie."

This was a real dilemma. If she continued to refuse, she risked looking ungrateful and would very likely embarrass Miss Vivien in front of the shop girl, but if she accepted, she would feel she was betraying her core value of not taking advantage of others.

Vivien seemed to notice her hesitation. "Please say yes so I can get on with enjoying myself."

Wasn't it part of her job to ensure Miss Vivien enjoyed her outing? "Well, when you put it like that, how can I refuse?" Anna couldn't deny, there was a thrill to owning something new, something that wasn't being handed off to her from one of her employers because they no longer wanted it. "But how can I ever repay you?"

Clasping Anna's hands together between hers, Vivien said, "Anna Maria, my friend, you've already repaid me just by being here."

Never before had her presence carried such value. Except when she was in the presence of Kingsley. He also had a way of making her feel valued, and appreciated, and even cherished. Anna took a deep breath, and felt truly grateful for Miss Vivien's show of kindness.

Anna turned back to look at herself in the mirror. "It does look quite nice."

"Of course. I have excellent taste," Vivien said, laughing.

105

"Far be it for me to disagree with you." Anna joined her in laughter.

"Box up her old hat," Vivien instructed the shop girl. "She's going to wear this one." Reaching up, Vivien removed her hat from her head. "I have to try on this rose hat one more time, just to be sure." As soon as the hat was placed upon her head, she asked Anna Maria, "How do I look?"

Miss Vivien would probably look fabulous in rags, but the tea rose hat looked particularly handsome on her. "You're beautiful, as always, and the hat looks good too."

"Anna Maria, you're the best. I knew it was a good idea to bring you along. Should I wear it?"

"I insist. If I'm to wear a new hat, you must too. And it looks perfect with what you're wearing."

"I thought so, too. It's one of the reasons I picked this outfit."

Miss Vivien finished purchasing both of the hats and instructed the shop girl to have the boxes holding their hats sent to out to her driver.

As they continued strolling along the main shopping street, looking into one store after the other, Anna Marie felt as if they were two of the best-dressed ladies in town. Clearly well-schooled in the art of charm and grace, Miss Vivien continued to put Anna at ease, never once making her feel uncomfortable, or unequal. To the contrary, it was one of the few times in her life she felt truly relaxed with someone outside her family.

As Anna and Vivien strolled from shop to shop admiring all the lovely items for sale, it was obvious Tarrytown catered to some of the wealthier families in the area. Many, no doubt, came into the village to do their summertime shopping. Of course, Anna couldn't afford to buy anything, but Vivien made window-shopping fun as they each pointed out the things they found most appealing. Interestingly, Miss Vivien didn't make any other purchases, and Anna didn't know if it was because there wasn't anything else she wanted to buy or because Miss Vivien didn't want to flaunt her wealth in front of her governess. Either way, Anna felt more at ease because of it. It seemed as though they really were two young friends out enjoying each other's company, rather than a wealthy debutante and a hired governess simply following her student around while she shopped.

As promised, they finished their outing back where they had started, and stepped into the Sweet Desires shop to enjoy warm cups of delicious hot chocolate. As they sipped their tasty treat, Vivien recalled several of the nicer pieces she had spied in the shops along Main Street.

"The only item I saw that really caught my eye was that fabulous black shawl with the vivid cabbage roses embroidered on it. I may have to think about coming back to get that, but not today. Today, my friend and I have new hats, and that is pleasure enough."

Never before had Anna felt so honored. In her time with the Goddards, Anna had seen enough visitors at Riverwood to know the family treated their guests in a more relaxed and casual manner than she had seen at the Dovers' in New York. Naturally, she had attributed their informal manners as an aspect of being in the privacy of their summer home, and not something they would normally do in public. But it seemed Miss Vivien was honestly reaching out to Anna in the kindest of ways. Such a show of friendship was wholly unexpected, but certainly not unpleasant, and Anna found she rather liked the idea of having Vivien as a friend.

But, of course, this wouldn't last. The moment they were back at Riverwood and under the watchful eye of Mrs. Goddard, Anna Maria would once again become Miss Lucci, the Italian governess, and Miss Vivien would return to being her student.

Chapter 10

Kingsley's journey to San Francisco was both boring and exciting, and in the final analysis, productive. Taking a long train trip to the West Coast was not his idea of a great way to spend his summer. Even with trade journals and an epic mystery novel to occupy his mind, the hours still had a way of seeming sluggishly slow.

If Miss Lucci could have accompanied him on this trip, it would be pure heaven, a true adventure. Though she had accused him of treating her like a servant he could freely take advantage of, he preferred to think of her as a friend, confidant, or even business assistant. However, servant or not, the rest of the world saw her simply as an unmarried woman. Unless she was his wife, the idea of traveling with her was so far beyond the realm of possibility, it was downright improper. With only Jamison, his valet, to keep him company, the hours dragged even as the grandeur of mountains and plains zipped by.

Upon arriving in the city on the Bay, he immediately made arrangements to take a behind-the-scenes tour of the Sutro baths. Though his guide made a concerted effort to make it all sound perfect, Kingsley had serious concerns about the size of the project and if it could continue to be profitable, or if it ever was, for that matter. From his observations, it appeared as though the project was overbuilt and underused.

The grand saltwater bathing house, built to serve the general public—and not an elite few—seemed a stunning example of overindulgence at the whim of a wealthy man. Though impressive, the space was excessive to say the least, with cases of oddities such as Egyptian mummies, stuffed animals, and an endless collection of seashells displayed throughout the upper floors.

Built to hold over twenty-five thousand guests, according to reports in the San Francisco papers, it rarely served more than four or five thousand visitors on any given day. Usually, far fewer than that. Sea water was notoriously corrosive on pipes and plumbing, and based on his calculations regarding the amount of power needed to heat the baths, the cost of ongoing repairs needed to keep the place running, and its low attendance, Kinsley predicted the baths would soon become too expensive to maintain. Adolph Sutro had poured significant funds into the project, hoping it would eventually pay off, but even a wealthy man could not subsidize a losing venture forever.

On the train ride back to New York, Kingsley began to compile his report and by the time he returned home was ready to hand it over to Max Branson for his review. Though not exactly encouraging, he did his best to present the facts in an unbiased manner, trusting his calculations would speak for themselves.

The following morning, when Kingsley met with Branson to discuss his findings, he voiced his concerns. Max listened with an attentive ear, and in the end, decided the Bailey Beach project either needed to be scaled back in size or it was doomed to encounter budget overruns and result in failed expectations. He did not want his firm attached to a losing venture and told Kingsley he planned to return to Newport to meet with the resort's investors.

"I must warn you, Kingsley, after I report your findings, we may find ourselves without a project to work on. Or at best, one much smaller than originally proposed. As attractive as the money may be, I rely too heavily on my Newport connections to be associated with an unprofitable venture. If Vanderbilt, Goelet, Oelrich, or any of the other Newport investors decide this project would make a mess of their summer resort, they'll cut me off without a glance."

"I'm sure you're right. Although I was looking forward to working with you, I understand your reluctance to endorse the project," Kingsley assured Max. Though he wasn't surprised by Max's reaction, the loss of the project was still disappointing. He had spent considerable time researching the Roman baths to prepare for the job, and now he was without work to keep him busy. "It looks as though I may be without a job for the foreseeable future. If that changes, I trust you'll let me know."

"You'll be the first person I contact," Max assured him. "I'd welcome another opportunity to work with you again. I trust your opinion completely."

"Good to know." While his financial security wasn't at risk, it went against his grain to be aimlessly unproductive. Still, this break in projects would give him an opportunity to spend more time at Riverwood with Miss Lucci. Except now, the need to translate the Italian reference book was much less urgent. Not that he necessarily needed to share that news with her. He was still interested in translating the Roman text book—if only for his own personal interests—and while they hadn't departed on the best of terms, he was still very much interested in working with Miss Lucci. Though the question remained, was she still willing to work with him?

Kingsley loved being an engineer—designing the inner workings of buildings as he solved logistical problems—and seeing the finished product. He had no regrets about not following his father into finance, none whatsoever. But lately, blueprints and plumbing diagrams weren't enough to hold his interest. He needed something, or someone, to fill the void, and he strongly suspected that someone was a certain Italian governess with lovely doe-like eyes.

The two men chatted a while longer. At the conclusion of their meeting, Kingsley made his way out to the street and turned north to head back home. He had only gone a block or two from Branson's office when he stopped to watch a large, cast iron bathing tub being hoisted to an upper floor of a twelve-story building. The workers were only using the building's single moving wrench and a thick rope to lift the load. From the effort being made by the men, and the lone horse doing the pulling, it looked as though the tub weighed a ton. Craning his neck to watch, Kingsley took a step closer to examine their setup. They were going about this all wrong. The arm of the wrench being used was too small to carry this much weight by itself. The workers should have linked their ropes to another hoist to help balance the load.

Stepping forward, he was just about to point out their mistake when the arm of the wrench gave way and the tub came plunging to the ground where Kingsley stood. Ducking and covering his arms over his head, he barely had time to react when he felt himself being hurled against the wall of the building. In the nick of time, he was pushed out of the way as the heavy tub crashed to the ground mere inches away, raising a cloud of dust. If not for the stranger's quick actions, Kingsley surely would have been seriously injured, if not crushed, by the falling tub. Instead, he'd only gotten the wind knocked out of him.

"Oh my goodness," Kingsley gasped, once he could catch his breath. "You saved my life."

"All in a day's work, my good friend. All in a good day's work. Timing is everything, you know." The man spoke with a refined accent and wore an expensive, dark grey suit. Reaching out a hand to assist him, the gentleman guided Kingsley quickly away from the accident site and the ensuing chaos.

Brushing the dust off his trousers, Kingsley said. "I owe you a debt of gratitude."

"Gratitude is always welcomed. Since I've done a good turn for you, maybe you can return the same to me.

"Anything within my power, you name it." Kingsley honestly meant what he said, feeling deeply obligated to repay this stranger. It wasn't necessarily an appealing idea, but the man had just saved his life. He would compensate him any way he could.

"I believe I saw you leaving Branson's office? I was on my way to see him. I'm looking for a mechanical engineer and am hoping he can recommend someone in the area."

"I'm a mechanical engineer," Kingsley said, almost without thinking.

111

"Well, now, you don't say? Have you any experience with commercial water works?"

"Not much," Kingsley said, in all honesty, "but I've done extensive study of the matter. As a matter of fact, that's why I met with Mr. Branson. We were working on a proposal for a large saltwater pool system, but it's not expected to move forward."

"Does that mean you're available?"

"I suppose it does, unless Branson confirms otherwise. What, exactly, do you have in mind?"

"Perhaps you'd like to join me at the Union Club for a drink and we can discuss this matter further. I prefer not to do business in the street, you understand." The man gestured for Kingsley to join him, and they began walking down the street together. "Name's Vanderzeit. Jules Vanderzeit," he said, offering his hand.

"Kingsley Goddard," he said, shaking the man's hand.

"Goddard? Any relation to Jayson Goddard?"

"He's my brother," Kinsley replied, wondering how this refined gentleman might know his lout of a brother.

Mr. Vanderzeit gave him a sideways glance. "I don't think we're referring to the same person. The man I'm thinking of is well over eighty."

"Then you must mean my grandfather, Jayson Goddard Senior."

"Worked in banking?" Mr. Vanderzeit asked.

"That's him. How do you know him?"

"It's a small world. I take it George Goddard is your father."

"Correct."

"Well, then, it seems you come from good connections. Are you George's eldest?"

"Correct, again." Manhattan was a relatively small world when it came to men of business, and Kingsley wasn't surprised Mr. Vanderzeit was well acquainted with his family. The bigger wonder was why he hadn't heard of Mr. Vanderzeit before, considering the man's knowledge of his family.

When they reached the Union Club, the doorman greeted them and ushered them inside. Since Kingsley was a member in good standing, he thought nothing of it, and expected Mr. Vanderzeit was also a member. It was probably the reason he was familiar with Kingsley's father and grandfather. They headed to the main meeting space, a room richly paneled in dark, mahogany woods. Large oil paintings covered the walls depicting hunting scenes, horse racing, and other manly pursuits.

After taking a quick look through the room, Mr. Vanderzeit picked a pair of thickly upholstered leather chairs at a table near the large, multipaned windows, well away from the polished bar and the tight group of men already gathered there.

"I must warn you," Mr. Vanderzeit said after they had taken their seats, "this may not be what you're expecting, but if you're interested in considering another project, I have a client in Italy who's looking to upgrade their water system. The project is quite extensive; it's for a large winery. They want to upgrade their irrigation, and water storage facilities, and install a new boiler, and full indoor plumbing. Would you be interested in overseeing the engineering of a project such as that?"

"A project in Italy? I've been thinking of taking a trip there. Maybe I can combine your business with my pleasure." Kingsley tapped his fingers on the table, his mind already abuzz with ideas.

"Well, I must say, this is good fortune. Always a pleasure when timing and intentions work together, wouldn't you agree?" Mr. Vanderzeit said, with an agreeable smile.

"Indeed, I would."

"Well, then, I guess it was most fortunate I saved your life back there, since I have need of your services."

"Very fortunate, indeed," Kingsley agreed, feeling slightly beholden to the fellow. "If I were to agree to take on this project, how long would I need to be in Italy?" he asked, thinking of Miss Lucci and his reluctance to spend more time away from her than he already had.

"Two or three months, at the least, although it could stretch to a year or more, depending on how quickly the project progresses. While my clients are anxious to upgrade their water system, the local labor is not always readily available to get the work done. But I can assure you, your time will be well compensated if you agree to accept this commission."

Kingsley wasn't overly worried about his salary, but being away from Miss Lucci for such an extended period did concern him. It made him wonder once again if there was a way to take her with him. Wouldn't that be grand!

They ordered drinks—a beer for Kingsley and a fine port for Mr. Vanderzeit—and spent the next half hour discussing the particulars of the project. By the time they parted ways, Kingsley had pretty much agreed to take on Mr. Vanderzeit's project. There were still a number of details to work out, including the exact schedule for Kingsley's travel to Italy, but Mr. Vanderzeit assured Kingsley he would be in touch.

This turn of events made Kingsley even more enthusiastic to return to Riverwood. Besides his desire to see Miss Lucci again, he was eager to share his good news with his family. However, more important than the loss of one job and the encouraging prospect of another, was his need to see Miss Lucci and set things to right between them. Their last time together had not gone nearly as well as he had hoped, and he had no intention of losing her as his working companion. Hopefully, if he could mend the pressure valve he'd broken when they were last together, he could get water flowing between them again, and move them further along towards something even more appealing than a mere working relationship.

CHAPTER 11

Soon after arriving at Riverwood, Kingsley spent the better part of an hour with his mother filling her in on his travels and news from New York. When she finally seemed satisfied she had heard all his news, Kingsley excused himself to seek out his sister, leaving Edith Goddard alone in the parlor to enjoy the view of the Hudson River through the large floor-to-ceiling windows.

As he exited the parlor to head upstairs, Kingsley was met by his sister. Perfect timing. Vivien had assured him she would look out for Miss Lucci and he was anxious to know what had happened while he was away. He wanted very much to speak with her in private. Kingsley gave a longing glance to the main staircase leading to the nursery on the upper floor of the house, but continued out to the gardens at the back of the house with his sister. As anxious as he was to see Miss Lucci, he felt it important to know what to expect, and asked Vivien to join him for a walk in the rose garden.

"Did you speak to Miss Lucci while I was gone?" Kingsley said as soon as they were far enough from the house to avoid being overheard.

"Of course I did. She's my governess," Vivien stated, walking calmly beside him.

"You know what I mean."

Vivien chuckled in that knowing way women had before answering. "I told her what a good man you are, but she had very little to say in return." Pausing along the path, she leaned forward to take in the scent of a delicate pink rose.

Darn, that didn't sound good. "I believe I may have offended her," Kingsley admitted. "Completely unintentional, of course." He supposed he shouldn't be surprised that his sister seemed uninformed. Miss Lucci was far too private of a person to reveal such an offensive encounter, especially to one of her charges.

Vivien straightened from the rose she'd been smelling. "Did something bad happen before you left?"

Kingsley shoved his hands in his pockets. "I took your advice and tried to make my feelings known, but she rebuffed me."

Vivien gasped. "You're kidding. I never would have suspected."

He turned to face his sister. "Did Miss Lucci say nothing?" Damnation. Kingsley should have kept his foolishness to himself.

"Come now, you can't be serious. Anna Maria refused you? What exactly did you do?"

"You needn't make it sound so lecherous. I only asked for a kiss goodbye, for good luck."

"You asked our governess to kiss you?"

"She's not my governess. She's my assistant."

"Regardless, she still works for you. Surely, you must know how strongly servants fear being mistreated by their employers."

"I feel bad enough as it is, I don't need you to remind me. I had hoped you were on my side."

"I am on your side, but what is she supposed to think? You don't even address her by her first name."

Kingsley leaned forward to examine a tightly closed bud, the last one on a lushly blooming bush of white roses. "Perhaps I've been a bit too formal." She had introduced herself as Miss Lucci, and he had let it go at that. But Vivien raised a good point. He had asked for a kiss before he had asked if he could address her by her given name. No wonder she had thought he was trying to take advantage of her. Until that day in the library, he hadn't done a good job of letting her know how he felt. Was it any wonder women had the upper hand when it came to courtship?

They were the ones who kept track of all these seemingly minor details, such as the date they met, or when and where they shared their first kiss.

Kingsley thought back to the day he had kissed Miss Lucci—Anna Maria. It had been the Tuesday before he left for San Francisco. Dang, it seemed he was going to need to take note of that.

"Calling her Miss Lucci seemed the right thing to do. I was trying to show her some respect." Shoving his hands in his trouser pockets, he continued along the garden path with Vivien at his side.

"Respect is all very well and good, especially for your tutor, but I had the impression you wanted more."

Oh, yes, he wanted more. A great deal more, but . . . "It seems I'm at a loss for how to go about letting her know?" Their first kiss had not gone well, except that he had enjoyed it more than he could say. Maybe, if he worked at it and didn't give up, there was a way to overcome his clumsiness. "Have you any suggestions?"

"As your sister, your *younger* sister, I'm surprised you would come to me for such advice. I would think you know this all by now."

"Yes, well, obviously, I've spent more time learning about the workings of pipes and boilers than I have about women. Look how badly my courtship with Consuelo ended."

"That was her mother's fault, not yours. Everyone knows Alva is a social climbing shrew. Unless you can add to her social standing, she'll run over you like you're nothing, because to her, that's what you are. It's why Mother will have nothing more to do with her, especially now that she's separated from her husband."

His sister was right. Since Alva's divorce from William Vanderbilt, Mother had refused to set foot in her grand Fifth Avenue chateau. But that was beside the point. Kingsley no longer cared what Alva or anyone else thought. His only concern was what Anna Maria thought.

"I never thought Consuelo was right for you. I don't believe she would have made you happy. She's too reliant on her mother's approval. Besides, having Alva Vanderbilt as your mother-in-law would have been a slow death. So tell me, what exactly did you say to Anna Maria when you left for San Francisco?" Vivien asked.

He was reluctant to admit his monumental blunder, even to Vivien.

"Come on, Kingsley, tell me," Vivien prodded. "I can keep your secret."

"As I said, I asked her for a kiss. A kiss for good luck." And what a spectacular kiss it had been. Until she had become offended, and broke it off. Not that he was going to share that bit of information with his sister. "But she accused me of trying to take advantage of her because she's a servant in my mother's house. As if that makes any difference to me."

"Oh, that's not good. At least you only asked her for a kiss. You didn't force yourself upon her, did you?"

"No, of course not. What do you think I am?"

As he recalled, she had freely agreed to kiss him, at least at first. It wasn't until he had taken the kiss deeper, hoping for more, that she had asked him to stop. Which he had. Never for a moment had he intended to force himself upon her.

"However, I am rather resigned to believe I've made a mess of all this. That's why I wanted to know if you were able to speak to her while I was gone. Did Jayson say or do anything to upset Miss Lucci?"

"No, I don't think Jayson bothered her while you were gone. He was too busy spending time in Tarrytown at the Drowned Duck drinking with Samuel Hoffman. I took Anna Maria shopping with me a couple of times. We had a lovely time together. I even bought her a hat."

"You bought your governess a hat? Didn't she think that was rather forward of you?"

"She did at first, but I convinced her it would make me happy, and she agreed. Besides, she went with me as my chaperone, not as my governess, and we became friends."

"Friends?" Growing up, Kingsley had never thought of his governesses, or even his tutors, for that matter, as his friends. And therein lay his problem. While he denied thinking of Miss Lucci as a servant, he had done very little to make her his friend. And yet, he always felt so comfortable in her company, as if they were the best of friends. Sadly, it seemed, Miss Lucci did not share his feelings on the matter.

"Yes, friends. The kind that talk to each other and share their feelings."

"Did she share her feelings about me?" Kingsley wondered.

"No, but I can't imagine she would. I am your sister. But I did detect some regret where you're concerned."

Regret! Did that mean she regretted leaving the library as she had? Did she regret rejecting him? Or did she regret that she had let him kiss her? Upon returning to Riverwood, his primary concern had been that Miss Lucci was still here, and that Jayson hadn't abused her. Would she even welcome his appeal for friendship? He wasn't sure how to go about such a task, but he was certainly willing to try.

"At least I still have the excuse of needing her help with the Italian translation," Kingsley spoke aloud, thinking it provided a perfectly good excuse for spending time with Miss Lucci. Although the need was less urgent, he saw no reason not to continue their sessions.

"Kingsley," Vivian strongly rebuked him. "I recommend you don't hide behind an excuse to see her again. Forget the Italian translation. You don't need a reason, you only need desire."

He stood in silence for a moment as he processed his sister's advice. "How do women know these things?"

"We have to. The security of our future depends upon it."

"I suppose you're right." Women needed to not only be pretty and accomplished, and witty, when it comes to men, they needed to weed out those with true potential from the merely ambitious.

~*~

The moment Kingsley returned to the house, he called for his valet. He had a plan, and it was time to put it into action. He had played the role of polite scholar for long enough. It was time to show Miss Lucci— Anna Maria—there was more to him than book learning and Italian translations.

Since returning from California, Kingsley had developed a new perspective on life. Maybe the act of stepping away from his life allowed him to see it more clearly. Or maybe his near brush with death from that falling bathtub had forced him to look beyond the moment and focus on what he wanted for his future.

Though born into a wealthy family, he often resented high society's self-proclaimed status of importance. He resented how often society's matrons felt they had the right to dictate over other people's lives, picking and choosing who was deemed good enough, and who was not.

When Jamison entered his room, he briefly discussed what he planned to wear to dinner, and then finished his instructions by saying, "When you're done here, I want you to find Miss Lucci and remind her I expect to see her in the library at five o'clock for our regular session together." He couldn't very well go chasing through the house to find Anna Maria, but Jamison could. What was the use of having servants if you couldn't use them from time to time to do your bidding?

Maybe, if he did something bold, as his sister suggested, he could regain some of his lost confidence, while returning to Miss Lucci's good graces. At least if he failed, there would be no one around to spread the tale. Of course, there was a difference between being confident and being arrogantly cocky. Confidence was admirable, while cocky was not.

CHAPTER 12

Anna Maria stepped into the library and all but closed the pocket doors, leaving the smallest gap between the two panels. For a split second, she wavered between closing them completely and opening them wider, and in the end, she left the doors as they were.

The first thing she noticed was that none of the study materials had been set out on the table where they usually sat. Signore Kingsley was already in the room, and was typically very good about having everything ready for them to begin their session together to make the most of their time together. But tonight, the first night after his return from California, instead of sitting at their work table as usual, he was sitting on a sofa with a tea service set out on the table next to him. It made her wonder if perhaps Jamison had made a mistake in delivering his message. It seemed as though Signore Kingsley was actually expecting someone else to join him.

He stood as she entered the room and greeted her halfway. "Miss Lucci, thank you for joining me."

"I was informed you wanted to resume our regular sessions, but it doesn't appear as if you're ready." Her eyes scanned the other tables in the room, but his Italian textbook was nowhere in sight.

"You're quite right. We won't be working on the translation tonight. If you don't mind, I'd much rather use our time together to simply speak together, in Italian." He gestured to the settee where he had been sitting. "*Per favore, siediti qui*," he continued. *Please, sit here.*

Feeling rather unsure of herself, Anna Maria crossed the room and sat with him on the settee as he had requested. He was so close, she could feel the touch of his shoulder and the brush of his thigh against hers. So close, she inhaled his tantalizingly musky scent with every breath she took. On a deeply womanly level, she was intensely aware of the tingling sensations racing along her spine and down to her toes, and touching all the soft, warm places in between.

Speaking in Italian as he had requested, she asked, "What do you wish to discuss?"

"The weather. How was your day? Anything two friends might think to discuss over tea."

He gestured at the service, and Anna took it upon herself to pour them each a cup as she spoke. "The weather has been quite pleasant, not too hot. My day went well. You missed our last play about the dinner party and the run-away cat. Miss Helen was excellent in the role of the maid. She has quite a gift for acting. Your mother is quite proud. Now we're working on one about Christopher Columbus. I thought it might be nice to include a history lesson with their Italian." Setting down the teapot, she asked, "How was your trip to San Francisco?"

"A little boring, all that train travel, but still a marvelous way to see how vast this country truly is. I'd love for you to see it someday."

Did he mean on her own, or with him? Either way, such an idea seemed highly unlikely. "Unless someone in San Francisco is in need of an Italian governess sometime soon, I don't expect to make such a trip." Anna giggled nervously as she handed Kingsley his cup of tea. She never giggled nervously.

He took a sip of his tea, then set down his cup before speaking. "I hesitate to bring up our last encounter, but it goes against my nature to leave an issue unresolved."

Anna was about to take a sip of her own tea, but stopped with the cup suspended in midair. Her initial thought was to deny any issue existed, but she quickly realized such a tactic would not work with

Signore Kingsley. Besides, denial was a coward's way, and she refused to be a coward.

"I suppose you're referring to the kiss we shared," she said in her most matter-of-fact voice before taking a sip of her tea. Hotter than she had expected, the brew slightly scalded the tip of her tongue, but she ignored the pain.

The slight lift of Kingsley's brow suggested he hadn't expected her to be so blunt. "So you agree, we *shared* a kiss."

"I know my actions were inexcusable. I have no defense for such improper behavior." Anna set aside her cup to wait for the beverage to cool.

"Your behavior was no more or less improper than mine," Kingsley stated adamantly. "I'm the one who owes you an apology. Please forgive me if I over-stepped my place. It was not my intention to take advantage of you or put you in an . . ." switching to English, he added, "awkward position."

Anna looked down at her hands, as if suddenly fascinated with her fingernails, which could use a good buffing. It hadn't been his fault she had given into temptation; she had wanted to kiss him. "It seems we both acted improper."

"I've never considered it improper for friends, especially close friends, to display affection for one another."

"Friends?" she blurted without thinking. She hadn't meant to react so strongly, but nothing about this encounter was as she expected.

"Considering the many hours we've spent together, should it not be possible, Anna Maria, for us to be friends?"

First Miss Vivien, and now Signore Kingsley. This was the second of the Goddard children who had asked for her friendship. What was it with these people? Did they not appreciate the proper boundaries between servants and their employers? "I don't recall giving you permission to use my given name."

"I would think, if we are to be friends, it should be allowed? And you needn't call me Signore. Kingsley will do just fine."

"And if I refuse?"

"Are you really so displeased with me?"

Displeased? Dear God, no. If anything, she was displeased with herself. "I can assure you, Signore Kingsley, you've not given me any reason to be displeased." *Ridiculously hopeful, and hopelessly romantic, but not displeased.*

"That's reassuring to hear, since I was wondering if you would be willing to take a ride with me into Tarrytown tomorrow?"

"That seems highly improper." Her hasty response was instinctive, but that didn't make it right. Could she not get past looking at everything as either proper or improper? She was starting to sound horribly redundant, as if it was the only thing that mattered. But it wasn't. There were other things to consider, such as how she felt, and what she wanted.

Covering her hands with his, he said, "I realize this is rather forward of me, but as you may have noticed, I don't always do what's proper where you're concerned. I would like to spend some time with you away from this house. Away from your duties as governess to my siblings. Not as my tutor or as my translator, but as my friend. Is that too much to ask?"

The warmth of his hands seeped through hers, winding its way up her arms and down her spine. It wasn't his words so much, but the seduction in his eyes that made her heart pound and blood rush to heat her skin. Never before had she received such a look from a man. And never before had she allowed herself to feel so hopeful.

"I can't help but worry what your family will think." One of them had to consider the impropriety of the situation, and apparently it wasn't going to be him. Men rarely bothered with such details, such as how an indecorous affair affected the standing of a servant in their house.

"I've thought about that. I doubt my siblings will care, but if anyone asks, I plan to say you're giving me another Italian lesson."

"I hardly see how that would justify me accompanying you into town? Everyone knows we conduct our lessons here in the library." Although, if anyone were to come upon them at this particular moment, it would hardly appear as if she were giving him an Italian lesson. Flirting with him, yes. Tutoring, not so much. If there were any instruction going on here, it was him teaching her in the ways of seduction. And from all appearances, she seemed a willing student.

"What if I told you there's a possibility I'll be taking a trip to Italy sometime soon, and I'd like to have an opportunity to practice speaking Italian outside our classroom?"

"Oh! You plan to go to Italy?" Which meant he would be gone for much longer than his trip to California. "Well, then your suggestion makes perfect sense." At least, she wanted to believe it did. How much merit his mother would assign to the situation was still questionable.

"So, will you accompany me into town as I have asked?"

Yes, she wanted to spend time with him, but the faint shred of sanity still lodged in her brain shouted for her to say no.

~~~

Kingsley sucked in a breath and held it as he waited for Anna to answer. Vivien was right. He was tired of doing the right thing. His whole life he had done what was expected of him as both his father's eldest son and a man of wealth and social standing. And what had it gotten him? More often than not, those he had hoped to impress had dismissed him as unimportant or unworthy of their consideration. It was time for him to do what was in his best interest, even if it wasn't exactly proper.

Obviously taken aback by his boldness, Anna said haltingly, "I'm not sure if I should."

Thank God, she hadn't said no. She might not have said yes, but at least she hadn't said no. It gave him a chance to convince her this wasn't such a bad idea.

"I'm not oblivious to our situation. I know *this* is considered improper on many levels." He gestured to the two of them. "But that's only because we've been told by others what's acceptable and what is not. No one ever thinks to ask what is best for us."

"For *us*?" Her doe-like eyes widened.

"Yes. Us." As the governess for his young siblings, his mother was basically her boss—and the wealthy never mixed with the servants for anything other than for what could be considered one-sided, abusive affairs—but by God, he cared for Anna Maria Lucci, and unlikely as it was, he wanted to believe she cared for him, too. Hoping against hope, he wanted to believe her kindness, and smiles, and gentle touch had nothing to do with his wealth and was more about her genuine care for him. And not just because she was paid to be his Italian tutor and translator.

As if to prove him right, Anna Maria laced her fingers with his. "Kingsley, I . . ."

He leaned forward, ready to take her in his arms, but paused. Although his resistance was wearing thin, the last thing he wanted to do was repeat his earlier mistakes.

She gazed into his eyes and didn't look away. "You're right. What you're suggesting isn't proper." Then, leaning closer, she added, "But I accept anyway."

It was all the encouragement he needed. Closing the gap between them, her kissed her. With all the passion burning through his bones, he pressed his lips against hers and wrapped her in his arms.

Heat shot right to his groin as a hot spark of pleasure sizzled through him. Her hand came up to rest firmly on his shoulders and her soft breasts grazed his chest. She smelled fresh and sweet, like talcum powder and lavender. Suddenly, the library seemed much smaller than before, as if the walls were closing in on them, encasing them in their own little world, apart from all that threatened to rule against them.

His hands were on the verge of roaming to places no mere friend should ever venture when she pulled back and ended their kiss. While her gesture was a firm indication this should go no further, the light in her eyes matched the brilliance of her luscious smile. "Should we continue to work on your Italian lessons now?" she asked sweetly.

"I'd rather not." It wasn't as if his mind could think clearly right now. Not with his heart racing, and his chest tightening as if compressed by a pressure valve. "If you don't mind, I'd much rather sit here and enjoy your company."

"All right," she said, still smiling. Scooting away ever so slightly, she picked up her teacup and took a sip. "Why don't you tell me more about this trip to Italy you have planned."

"I'd rather not say too much. Not yet, until the project is final. But I'd love to tell you about San Francisco. And the Rocky Mountains. You should see the Rocky Mountains."

The rest of the hour whizzed by and before he knew it, the clock struck six, signaling the end of their time together. If it weren't for the fact that he didn't want his family to come looking for him, he would have gladly spent the rest of the evening ensconced in the library with Anna Maria. Knowing there were some formalities that needed to be maintained, he reluctantly let her return to her classroom while he joined his family for dinner.

~*~

The following morning, Kingsley had the finest horse and carriage in his father's stables brought around to the graveled drive. He was taking Anna Maria riding into Tarrytown, and they would be leaving by the front door. He would not have her sneaking round from the backdoor servant's entrance. He was taking her riding, and like any house guest to their summer home, he wanted to see her using the front door.

He was standing in the entrance foyer, awaiting her arrival, when his mother walked into the room.

"Going somewhere?" she asked as she glided toward him in a swish of mint green skirts and floral scents.

"Yes, as a matter of fact. I'm taking a ride into town." He glanced up at the staircase, wondering what was keeping Anna Maria, while at the same time, grateful for her delay. Before this, she had always been so punctual, but as he had observed once before, women seemed to enjoy keeping men waiting in social situations, as opposed to the business-like meetings they had conducted before.

"Do you need company? Perhaps one of your sisters would like to join you."

"That won't be necessary. Miss Lucci is accompanying me."

"Miss Lucci!" If the tone of her voice hadn't indicated her stark surprise, the look in her eyes certainly would have. "I'm not sure I approve of this."

Thankfully, he was prepared for any disapproval his mother might want to voice. "If I am to live in Italy for any amount of time, I'd like to converse without stumbling for words. I suggested Miss Lucci accompany me into town to coach me on common conversations I may expect to encounter upon arriving in a new country and she graciously agreed to assist me."

"Sort of like role playing?" his mother asked, looking much more pleased by the idea.

"Exactly."

"I think that's a marvelous idea. No better way to understand the role you're to play than to expose yourself to it in real life. I almost wish I could come along and watch."

Never would he allow his mother to join them.

"Unfortunately, I'm expecting Mrs. Delafield and Mrs. Beaumont here for lunch this afternoon," she continued.

Kingsley breathed a sigh of relief. "I think it's best if I take my lessons, and make my mistakes in private, without the benefit of an audience. I'm sure you never allowed outsiders to sit in on your rehearsals when you were in the theater."

"Never. Our director would never have allowed it. Even your father was not allowed to visit during rehearsals. But as I recall, I only performed in one other play after we met. He was so insistent on taking me away from the theater life, I had very little time to even consider such a thing."

Such a revelation didn't surprise Kingsley. He doubted his father had wanted his future wife performing for the good folks of New York simply because they could afford the price of a ticket. From what Kingsley had heard, after his grandfather, Jayson Goddard, had reluctantly agreed to the marriage, he had also insisted on a rather brief engagement for his son and Miss Edith Marshburn, followed by a smallish wedding, which was followed by a long honeymoon in Paris.

The thinking behind it all was that by the time his parents returned to New York, society would have moved on to other more recent and succulent gossip to entertain themselves and the brief theatrical history of his bride could easily be forgotten. For the most part, it had worked. While it was no secret within the family, rarely was Edith Goddard's past as an actress brought up in polite company.

Once again, Kingsley glanced up the main staircase, wondering what was keeping Anna Maria. It also seemed his mother was in no hurry to be on her way and was prepared to stand with him while he waited. "I expect you have things to do before your guests arrive," he offered, hoping his mother would go on her way. While he'd been forthcoming about his intent to have Miss Lucci accompany him into town, he had no desire to witness a confrontation between his mother and Anna Maria.

"Not really. Most everything is already prepared. We'll be lunching on the terrace."

"Really? Have you had a look outside? The wind seems to be picking up. It may not bode well for an outdoor event. You may want to check with cook about moving it into the sun porch." Though he had no idea what the wind was doing, if it would send his mother on her way, he would claim they were expecting snow.

"I do hope that's not the case. The terrace provides a much better view of the river. I so want to impress Mrs. Delafield. It's her first visit to Riverwood. You know how important it is to cultivate good relationships with the right sort of people."

Though he knew the answer, Kingsley felt a need to resist his mother's comment. "Oh, really. Do tell, what sort of people is that?"

Mother shot him a disdainful look. "Don't be difficult, Kingsley. It doesn't suite you. You know very well whom I mean. Mrs. Delafield and her daughter, Mrs. Beaumont, are well-connected members of New York society. They're coming to discuss the theme for this year's Women's Assistance League holiday ball, and with my theatrical background, I want to offer my assistance. It will be quite an honor to be on their decorating committee."

She continued to stand there as if determined to see him off. Just then, out of the corner of his eye, he spied Anna Maria leaning over the banister and peering down at him. It seemed she was hesitant to come down while his mother was there, and his mother seemed in no hurry to leave.

"I just remembered, I want to bring along my notebook, to take notes, of course, and I've left it in the library," Kingsley stated loudly, hoping his voice would carry up the staircase. "I'll walk with you to the back of the house on my way to fetch it." He held out his arm for his mother to take.

"Isn't that nice of you. I suppose I should take a look at the terrace before my guests arrive. I would hate to have napkins flying across the yard, if it's as breezy as you say."

"Yes, Mother. It's not like you to leave such details to the last minute. It best to be sure." He walked with her toward the back of the house, sending her on her way when they reached the hall leading to the library. The moment he was out of her sight, he dashed into the library, picked up his notebook, which he really didn't need, then dashed back around through the smoking room to reach the front foyer just as Anna Maria was descending the stairs. He was nearly out of breath by the time he met her at the front door.

"Are we ready to go?" she asked, as if nothing was amiss.

"More than ready." After setting down his notebook on a nearby table, Kingsley reached for her hand to escort her out the front door and down the broad porch to the waiting carriage.

~*~

They were walking down the main shopping street of Tarrytown, when Kingsley stopped to examine some items on display in the window of a jewelry store. Standing beside him, Anna could see his reflection in the glass. The image was one of a stunningly handsome man in a white linen suit with his jaunty straw hat slipped slightly to one side. To her eyes, he was the best-looking man in town.

As she continued to observe him, it seemed Kingsley had his eye on a particularly striking watch displayed in the store window. When he leaned slightly toward her, she expected him to point it out to her, as if she hadn't already noticed his intense interest. Instead, in flawless Italian, he said, "Would it be wrong of me to want to kiss you again?" There was a hint of laughter in his voice, and when she caught his eye in the window, a noticeable gleam.

"*Qui? Sulla strada?*" she asked. *Here! On the street?* His bold question almost had her swaying into his arms, but she remained properly upright.

"*Si, proprio qui, adesso.*" *Yes, right here, right now*. The intensity of his look caused her to catch her breath. He was serious.

This was so like Kingsley to push the limits of what was proper. To do something so rash would surely put them at risk of being spied, but his ardent attention had her questioning her resistance.

"Would it be so bad?" he asked, as if speaking her thoughts aloud.

Anna glanced about the street. While no one in the area looked familiar to her, in a town of this size, it was very likely there were many who knew Kingsley and the Goddard family. She took a half step away and stated, "We may be seen, and we can't have that." *What would Mrs. Goddard say if she were to hear about such a public display of affection?*

"No, I suppose we can't," Kingsley quipped, taking a step closer. "It's probably best if you keep your distance, or I may be taken in by your beautiful eyes and sparkling smile."

"You think my eyes are beautiful?" Anna asked, feeling ridiculously naïve as she backed up against the jewelry store. If they kept this up, surely someone would come out from the store and shoo them away for causing a disturbance.

"Like rich melted chocolate, I could drown in them, and die a happy death."

Now he was just being silly, but Anna Maria found she rather liked it. "Before you take your last breath, I think it would be best if we returned to your carriage."

"But we haven't even had lunch."

Oh, yes, lunch. The reason they had come into town. Or at least one of them. "That's right. You promised me a meal in exchange for tutoring you in Italian."

"In exchange for your company, but you're right. We should head over to the Crescent Moon. Perhaps I should hold your hand."

"Absolutely not!" A governess did not hold hands with a man on a public street.

"I wouldn't want you to slip on these cobble stones," he said with a look that was all innocence.

She pretended to consider his offer. "I will take your arm, if you insist, but I shall not hold your hand. Not while we're in public."

"Ah, does that mean you will when we're in private? Say the privacy of my carriage?"

She couldn't hold back the smile teasing her lips. "Perhaps. If lunch is good."

"I have no control over how well the chef prepares our food."

"But you did pick the restaurant."

"And they've never let me down, but still, you wouldn't deny a hungry man, would you?"

"All right, but only if you behave yourself during lunch." Never before had Anna allowed herself to flirt so outrageously with a man, or enjoyed anything more.

"Certainly, now that you've given me something to look forward to." Taking her hand, he placed it safely in the crook of his arm, and together they strolled merrily down the street.

~*~

Sighing contentedly, Anna relaxed against the cushioned bench of the carriage as they rode along the Hudson River on the road back to Riverwood. She couldn't recall a finer day. They had lunched at the Crescent Moon teahouse, and true to her word, she had allowed him to hold her hand as they walked back down Main Street to the River Park where Kingsley's carriage was waiting to take them back home.

They had just turned onto the road that would take them back to Riverwood when Kingsley quite unexpectedly said, "I want you to go to

Italy with me. If I get that new job, I want you there, with me. With you by my side, I know I could do great things. Together, we'll see great sights. You'll be my interpreter."

His interpreter! He couldn't be serious. This was not what Anna wanted to hear. It made her wonder if all his flirting had only been a ruse to ensure she would do his bidding. The last thing she wanted was to travel by his side as a mere interpreter. Pulling her hand from his, she stated, "Your Italian is perfectly acceptable. You should have no problems on your own." She had no desire to return to Italy. Not unless she could be assured she would be allowed to return to her job in New York with Mrs. Goddard, and she doubted Mrs. Goddard would accept her back if she accompanied her son unchaperoned.

"But, I want you there," Kingsley insisted, taking back her hand.

"I will not travel as your servant," Anna stated firmly. Really, did she need to spell it out for him? After all, they were currently speaking English. Surely, he understood her meaning.

"My servant! Oh, no, Anna Maria. You misunderstand. I don't want you to be my servant. I want you to be my wife."

"Excuse me?" *Your wife?* Had Kingsley just asked her to marry him? Anna Maria's heart leapt and fell in a single beat. Mrs. Goddard would never allow such a thing, and she found it hard to believe Kingsley would so strongly disappoint his family. "Please, do not play with my feelings."

"I'm perfectly serious." The look in his eyes supported what he was saying.

It seemed too good to be true. To think the man of her dreams might actually love her enough to want to marry her was more than she could hope. "You wish to marry me?" she asked, sounding as dazed as she felt.

"Of course, I do. What do you think these past few days have been about? Surely, you must know I love you. I want you to be my wife." A smile of undisguised joy played across his wonderfully handsome face, while his eyes seemed lit from within.

Still, it was hard to believe a rich man such as Signore Kingsley could ever honestly wish to marry a governess employed by his mother. "Your mother will never agree."

"You may have noticed, I come and go as I please. I stopped relying on my parents' approval some time ago. If it was up to my father, I would be in banking, not getting my shoes dirty trekking around building sites. I want to build things, Miss Lucci, including a life with you."

Anna forced herself to breathe as she considered his words. Although he seemed honestly earnest in his request, she had never allowed herself to dream Signor Kingsley would ever care for her as she did for him. Still sorting out the thoughts spinning through her head, she managed to say, "You wish to build things, Signore Kingsley?" Unable to hold it all in, a hopeful smile slipped past her lips.

"A life with you, Anna Maria, if you will allow me."

Until this moment, she hadn't dared to think this could happen. She'd been so sure of her station in life, and just as sure of her opinions and judgments supporting her assessment of his elite world. And yet, the risk of remaining firmly lodged in her tight, narrow viewpoint was far greater than the risk of believing in something better for herself.

"Will you marry me, Anna Maria?" Kingsley asked with a look of hopeful expectation.

Happy tears misted her eyes. "Yes, Signore Kingsley. I'd be happy to be your wife."

"Then, if you wouldn't mind, could you please stop calling me Signore? Kingsley will do well enough."

Anna Maria laughed. "Certainly, Kingsley." She laughed again, overcome with both nerves and joy. "Kingsley," she stated again, getting used to the idea that she would someday soon be his wife. Mr. and Mrs. Kingsley Goddard. Anna Maria Goddard. Yes, she liked the sound of that very much.

"May I kiss you now, Anna Maria?"

"I should certainly hope so, if I am to become your wife."

He pulled her close and kissed her with such desire, she was certain her toes would burst out of her shoes, they curled in such delight. And he kept kissing her, and touching her, and holding her tight for the remainder of the ride, until they turned onto the drive that led to Riverwood. Only then did they both pull away and make an effort to straighten their clothes and set things right. Anna reached up to make sure her hat was still in place, certain it had been knocked off kilter during their lovemaking. After a slight adjustment and tucking up of several stray strands, she hoped she looked presentable.

"Do you think anyone will know?" she asked shyly, certain she must look remarkably different now that she was engaged to be married.

"You look fine. I doubt anyone will suspect a thing. But won't they be surprised?"

To say the least. In all likelihood, his mother would be furious. "When do you expect to tell them?" Anna suddenly felt a pang of remorse, as if her fairy tale romance was about to end.

"I'll wait until we're all gathered for Sunday dinner. It'll give me time to make arrangements for you to join us at the table."

"Join you for Sunday dinner?" She had strong doubts Mrs. Goddard would ever allow a servant, even a governess, to sit at her table. All her old worries about this being a doomed affair rose to the surface.

But once again, Kingsley's roguish smile and boyish charm had a way of setting her fluttering mind at ease. "Trust me, Anna Maria. I'll handle everything. You've nothing to worry about. You've agreed to be my wife, and I plan to hold you to your word. Anything less would be improper."

CHAPTER 13

It was a sugar sweet sunrise and Anna Maria was over the moon with happiness as thoughts of Kingsley frolicked in her brain. If all went as Kingsley planned, by the end of the week she would no longer be a governess. She would be his fiancée. They already had an understanding. She simply needed to wait until he made the big announcement to his family. Then she would shed this old life and step into her new one with Kingsley Goddard. Of course, she wasn't exactly sure how it was all going to work, but Kingsley had assured her he would take care of everything, and she believed him.

Nearly bouncing as she walked, Anna was on her way to the classroom to prepare for her day with the children. Her joy was so apparent, she wondered how she could ever keep from revealing her good news with the younger Goddards, especially Vivien, who seemed particularly perceptive when it came to a person's emotions. She was about to enter the classroom when she was stopped by Mrs. Goddard's personal maid.

"Mrs. Goddard asks to see you in her private sitting room. You're to go there now." Louisa informed her. Though she wasn't close with Mrs. Goddard's maid, Louisa's tone of voice seemed harsher than usual.

"Her private sitting room? Are you sure?" Suddenly her feet felt stuck to the hall carpet. This had to be serious. Never before had Anna been called into Mrs. Goddard's private chambers. She wondered if

Kingsley had already spoken to his mother and she was calling her in to congratulate her? Or ask about her wedding plans? But based on the sinking feeling she had in the pit of her stomach, and the look of disapproval on Louisa's face, her instincts told her that wasn't the case.

"I'm certain. She's there, waiting for you." Louisa waved her hand as if to shoo Anna on her way.

Managing to get her feet to move as they should, Anna turned back to the servants' staircase and made her way to the family's private rooms.

When she stepped into Mrs. Goddard's sitting room, she saw the mistress of the house was not alone. Mrs. Bernice Dorvall was with her. Anna had met the woman once or twice before and was very fond of the lady for the kind and gentle manner in which she addressed everyone, including the servants of the house. The moment Anna stepped into the room, she knew something was wrong. Mrs. Goddard seemed noticeably agitated, drumming her hands on the arms of her chair as if unable to contain their motion. Mrs. Dorvall also had a look of anxious anticipation, as if she were uncomfortable with what was about to happen. Anna stood stiffly, waiting to hear what Mrs. Goddard had to say.

"Miss Lucci, this a rather disagreeable duty I must perform, but it has come to my attention that you have engaged in an indecorous flirtation with Kingsley while tutoring him, here in my own home. From what I hear, I suspect you may have taken this flirtation seriously. Surely, you understand, this cannot be allowed to continue."

Mrs. Dorvall sank back in her chair as her eyes popped wide in a look of pure astonishment. A second later, she schooled her expression to one of shocked detachment, and Anna had the feeling she was painfully embarrassed by Mrs. Goddard's alarming show of social superiority.

Anna Maria raised her head proudly, every nerve in her body taut with embarrassment and anger. "Have you spoken with Signore Kingsley?"

Mrs. Goddard dismissively shook her head. "My son is simply acting as young men do. If you wish to continue in my employment, for your own good, you must cease this flirtation at once."

Anna Maria was too shocked to know what to say. Never had she expected Mrs. Goddard to accuse her in such a manner. It stung even more to have Mrs. Dorvall witness the accusation. What was it with these rich people that they should need an audience when reprimanding their servants.

Seemingly unaware of Anna's distress, Mrs. Goddard continued, "Surely, you must have known how dangerous your actions were." With an added measure of disgust, she added, "And how shameful. As a governess, you can't expect anything to come of this."

"How can you say that? He asked me to marry him," Anna blurted out, too angry to hold her tongue.

"Nonsense. He was only flirting with you," Mrs. Goddard insisted.

"You are wrong. You think he does not mean it when he tells me he loves me, but you are wrong. I know Signore Kingsley would not lie to me."

"It really doesn't matter. Nothing can come of this. Marriage with my eldest son is impossible. Kingsley's only interest was learning Italian to aid his research. You've been most helpful, but he can't marry you."

Anna took a deep breath, attempting to hold back her anger. She had already said more than she had intended. She would not give Mrs. Goddard the pleasure of seeing her lose her temper. With all the dignity she could muster, she quietly stated, "That is for Kingsley to decide."

"He is a Goddard. I will not have him marry a governess." Mrs. Goddard began to raise her voice, while Mrs. Dorvall silently recoiled with a look of stunned disapproval. Mrs. Goddard's guest seemed as shocked as Anna by this horrid display of condemnation.

Anna kept her head held high. "Kingsley has asked me to marry him," she repeated.

Mrs. Goddard slapped the palm of her hand on the arm of her chair. "It was merely a flirtation. Inappropriate perhaps, but nothing more."

"You are wrong," Anna Maria insisted. Mrs. Goddard had to be wrong. She couldn't stand to think Kingsley had lied to her, using her emotions to make a fool of her after she'd been so vigilant to avoid such a thing.

"Trust me. I am not wrong. Kingsley will not marry you. Not now. Not ever. If you insist on perpetuating this fantasy, be advised, I will dismiss you from this house without the benefit of a reference."

"I can assure you, Mrs. Goddard, that won't be necessary." Turning on her heel, Anna Maria stalked out of the room. She had no desire to stay where she was not wanted. The moment she was out in the hallway, she quickened her pace.

Fearing she might run into one of the other staff, she rushed as swiftly as she could up the back stairs to her room. After closing the door with an angry whoosh, she locked the latch. Only then did she sink onto her bed and let herself cry. Her face scrunched so tight with emotion, it hurt. When she awoke that morning, she had believed she was falling in love; now, after speaking with Mrs. Goddard, she was falling apart. Angry, hurt and sad, it bothered her to no end how easy it was for those people—those rich, entitled people—to shatter her dreams and break her heart.

She had thought she was loved, accepted, and appreciated for who she was, but Mrs. Goddard had firmly put an end to such thoughts. What an idiot she'd been to allow herself to believe she was worthy of being loved by Signore Kingsley, worthy to be his wife. Obviously, as Mrs. Goddard had just pointed out, she'd been wrong. She was simply the Italian governess, hired to do a job that didn't include getting friendly with her employer's son, much less fall in love.

But she wouldn't be broken, not by *them*. Everything happened for a reason, and surely this was God's way of reminding her of her place in the world. She'd been foolish to think a man of wealth would seriously consider marrying a woman of her rank. A woman who needed to work for her living and whose father was merely a merchant back in her hometown in Italy.

Mrs. Goddard was right, it had been a dangerous flirtation. Dangerous for her, but not for Kingsley. Men such as he were above condemnation. Undoubtedly, this incident would be seen as nothing more than a moment of weakness on his part. The rich always got what they wanted and came away no worse off than if it had never happened. But she, Anna Maria Lucci—a mere governess—she would be accused of being a gold-digger, or even worse.

With or without references, it was impossible to stay in this house. To do so would require her to acknowledge she had acted inappropriately, but she had done nothing wrong. Right from the beginning, she had known it was wrong to give in to her attraction to Kingsley, but he had done a good job of fooling her into believing they could be together, and she worst of all, she had believed them. Only a fool believed the wealthy would marry one of their servants. Hadn't she learned from Mrs. Dover? The moment a servant was no longer needed or wanted, they were discarded without a moment's hesitation.

She would not stay where she was not wanted, and she had no desire to see Signore Kingsley again anytime soon. Surely, he would only tell her more lies, as surely as he had duped her into believing he cared.

Enough was enough, and she'd had more than enough of these snobby, rich people telling her what to do and where to go. If it were at all possible, she would return to Italy as soon as she was able. Being frugal to the bone, since her arrival in America she had saved every dollar she could. Hopefully, she had enough to buy her passage back home. Even if it meant traveling in third class steerage, she was determined to leave New York and never look back.

Standing, Anna Maria pulled a handkerchief from her pocket and hastily wiped the tears from her face. She knew what she had to do. In less than twenty minutes, she packed her meager possessions in her traveling bag and was heading down the back stairs toward the servants' hall. Without stopping to explain herself, or bid her fellow staff goodbye, she exited through the kitchen door and hurried toward the carriage house. Hopefully, Mr. Miller, the head groomsman, would agree to take her to the train station so she could return to New York. It was the least these people could do, since they had been the ones to bring her out to their remote summer home.

Before she reached the wide-open doors to the stable, an expensive looking carriage pulled up the drive from the front of the house at a break-neck speed. Anna had to scurry out of the way to avoid being run down. *How rude*, she thought. *Have they no care for where they're going or who they might run over?*

The carriage stopped a few feet from Anna and a groomsman hopped off the back to open the door. Anxious to be on her way, she was about to turn away when the groomsman called out to her. "Signorina Lucci, if you please, Mr. Vanderzeit would like a word with you."

Mr. Vanderzeit! She hadn't heard from him since the day she left Italy. "Mr. Vanderzeit is here?" she asked.

"Yes, in the carriage, Miss, if you don't mind," the groomsman said.

She needed a ride to the train station. Hopefully, he would take her there. Determined to ask, she climbed into the carriage with her traveling bag. As she took a seat on the backward facing cushion, Anna was stunned to see Mrs. Dorvall sitting next to Mr. Vanderzeit.

"Mrs. Dorvall! Forgive me, but what are you doing here?" The shock of seeing the woman who had just witnessed her set-down was quite disconcerting. And why was Mr. Vanderzeit suddenly here in her company?

"I want to help," Mrs. Dorvall replied just before the carriage lurched forward and made a wide turn out of the drive.

Darting a glance between Mr. Vanderzeit and Mrs. Dorvall, Anna asked, "Does that mean you'll take me to the train station?"

"We'll do better than that," Mr. Vanderzeit told her. "We'll take you all the way to New York, and get you a place to stay."

"I don't understand. Why would you do that? Why are you here?"

Mrs. Dorvall reached out a gloved hand and rested it on Anna's. "I'm happy to help. My husband Richard owns the Park View Hotel. We'll give you a room there until you know what to do next. It will be no problem."

"I can't afford a room in the Park View Hotel." She wasn't even sure if she had enough money to buy her passage back to Italy.

"You needn't worry. You'll be my guest," Mrs. Dorvall assured her.

"But why? Why would you do this for me?" Mrs. Dorvall's offer was shockingly generous, but if she were truly serious, this would solve a number of Anna's problems. At least, for the moment.

Mrs. Dorvall exchanged a knowing look with Mr. Vanderzeit before she answered. "Jules and I agree it's the right thing to do. I think it's appalling how Edith handled your situation. I'm sure she thinks she's doing what is best for Kingsley, but she seems to have forgotten the passion of young love. I have every faith Kingsley didn't lie to you, or deceive you. If he told you he loves you, and wishes to marry you, I'm sure it's true."

Thank God, someone believed her. "This is so very kind of you, but I still don't understand why you should take an interest in me. And excuse me for asking, Mr. Vanderzeit, but what are you doing here? The last time I saw you was in Italy."

"Rest assured, I've been keeping a close eye on your situation. I would never leave one of my charges unguarded or unprotected."

Whatever could he mean? As far as she knew, until this moment, Mr. Vanderzeit had never been a visitor at the Goddard home.

~*~

It was a glorious summer day and Kingsley had spent much of the morning riding along the river. He had also spent much of the morning, and all of last night, thinking about how to tell his family about his engagement. He expected Vivien, and maybe Father, would be happy for him. But his mother, as well as Jayson, were likely to be less accepting. Either way, it really didn't matter. Regardless of their opinions, he was determined to make Anna Maria his wife.

Upon returning to the house, he quickly changed and then headed off to the classroom, thinking he would spy on his favorite governess. It was nearly the lunch hour and he planned to ask Anna Maria to join him for a picnic out by the river. He had already made arrangements with the cook to prepare him a basket, but when he got to the classroom, no one was there.

They must have ended their session early. He wondered where they could have gone. He was on his way to the library, thinking Anna Maria might be there, when he saw his mother's maid.

"Excuse me, Louisa," Kingsley stopped the maid as she rushed down the hall, "have you seen Anna, umm, I mean Miss Lucci? She's not in the classroom. Where is everyone?"

"Forgive me, Mister Kingsley," the maid said, nervously twisting her apron in her hands, "but I think it would be best if you asked your mother."

"My mother? Why would she know? Is something wrong?"

"Sir, I cannot say, but I'm sure Mrs. Goddard would like to see you. She's in the drawing room," Louisa informed him.

With determined strides, Kingsley marched through the house. Upon finding his mother in the drawing room, he immediately asked, "Has something happened? I was looking for Miss Lucci and Louisa told me you would know where to find her."

"It seems Miss Lucci has decided to leave our employment."

"Leave our employment? Why on earth would she do that?" He had just asked her to marry him, and she had agreed. What could possibly have happened to change all that.

"I know she's been working with you, but I found her behavior inappropriate for a governess in my house."

"You can't be serious!" Much as he tried to keep it under control, his ire started to grow. He didn't like where this conversation was going, not one bit.

"A woman in her position should respect the boundaries between us and them. I'll not have a servant in my house flirt with one of my boys."

One of her boys! For God's sake, he was a grown man. "Do you realize, I've asked her to marry me?"

More stern-faced then he'd ever seen her, his mother looked as though she were ready to scream. "What on earth possessed you to act

143

so impulsively – especially on a matter of such importance? You know better than that. Our family's social reputation is at stake here."

"Reputation!" *To hell with their sacred reputation.* "What about *my* happiness?"

"Happiness is fleeting. Marriage is forever. Or at least it should be. You're my eldest son. I won't have you married to a woman with no social standing. Think what it will do to me, and to your father. Can you even imagine how a scandal such as this will disappoint your father?"

"I cannot believe you would do this to me. You were an actress when Father married you. How is that so much better than an educated, Italian governess?"

Mother gasped. "Kingsley! How can you say such a thing? I'm your mother."

Kingsley regretted his insult—he knew better than to bring up his mother's background—but damn it, she had no right to meddle as she had done. Especially not without speaking with him first. As her son, he deserved such respect. *What the hell was she thinking?* "I'm sorry if I've hurt your feelings, Mother, but think how Anna Maria must feel."

"I really don't care how she feels. I won't have you flirting with your governess as if you were some love-struck lad in knee breeches. You're a grown man."

"Correct. Old enough to make my own choices." He turned away intent on leaving her presence. If he stayed much longer he would say something truly unkind.

"Where do you think you're going?" his mother called out to him.

Good manners forced him to respond. "To find Anna Maria, of course."

"You can't be serious."

"Never more so."

"Oh, please, Kingsley, be real. How long do you plan to continue with this . . . this little affair of yours?"

He glared at his mother with a satisfied grin. "Until she says yes and becomes my wife, if I should be so lucky."

Thinking only of Anna Maria, Kingsley dashed out the door and headed for the servants' hall. Hopefully, someone there would know where she had gone.

Before he had reached the back of the house, he met up with Vivien. "Are you looking for Anna Maria?" she asked.

"Yes. Do you know where she is?"

"I heard what Mother did, and I saw Miss Lucci leave with Mrs. Dorvall. I expect she gave her a ride into town. She may be headed to New York. You should start there."

"New York? Why in the world would she go there?"

"Where else should she go? She and Mother had quite a fight. She couldn't stay here."

"I need to find her." He gave her a quick hug and kiss on her cheek. "Thanks. It's nice to know I have someone on my side."

"I'm sure Mother will agree once she understands how important this is to you."

"You have far more confidence in her than I do, but I certainly don't plan to stand around and waste my time while I try to explain it to her."

Before Vivien could answer, Kingsley was on his way out the door and headed toward the stables. He was not about to give up or give in. He had given up Consuelo when Mrs. Vanderbilt had refused his proposal, and had willingly given up on the Bailey Beach project when questioned by Max about its profitability, but by heaven he refused to give up on Anna Maria simply because his mother didn't approve.

If she really wanted nothing to do with him, he would let her go, but until he heard such words from her directly, he was determined to pursue her to the ends of the earth if necessary. He had to find Anna Maria. He couldn't let her go. She was the best woman he had ever known, better than all the rest. Better than Consuelo Vanderbilt, or any of the other women high society might deem appropriate. Anna Maria was the one for him. Without her, nothing felt right.

CHAPTER 14

Having missed the last train out of Tarrytown, Kingsley was forced to wait until the following day to travel to New York. Too angry to spend another evening in the presence of his mother, he made arrangements to spend the night at the Riverside Inn, one of the finer hotels in the village. He also hired a messenger to instruct his valet to pack a bag and join him at the inn. He couldn't very well travel to Manhattan with only the clothes on his back. Of course, if all had gone as he had hoped, he would have already been on his way instead of pacing through his suite of rooms in this sleepy resort village.

Too upset to relax, he couldn't help but worry about Anna Maria. Vivien had seen her accept a ride from Mrs. Dorvall, and the head groomsman had confirmed they had driven off in the direction of Tarrytown. It only made sense that Mrs. Dorvall had returned to New York—she didn't have a home in the area—and hopefully the kind lady had seen it in her heart to provide Anna Maria with transportation back to the city. But then what? Where would she stay? As far as he knew, she had no family to speak of in America. Where would she go? What would she do?

This not knowing was infuriating, made only worse by the frustration of wasted hours waiting for the morning train out of Tarrytown. All because his mother hadn't taken the time to speak with him first before she falsely accused Anna Maria of improper behavior.

Good Lord, Anna Maria didn't have an improper bone in her body. It was he who had pursued her, not the other way around.

Just as he turned to pace the room for the dozenth time, there was a knock on the door. When Kingsley opened it, he was surprised to see Vivien standing in the hall with Jamison.

"What are you doing here at this time of night?" Kingsley asked his sister.

"I've come to tell you Mother feels awful about what she's done," Vivien said, brushing past Kingsley as she stepped into the room.

Not wishing to discuss his love life in front of his valet, Kingsley sent Jamison to the other room to unpack his bag. When the valet was gone, he said, "I find it hard to believe she's suddenly had a change of heart."

"I'm not sure I would go quite that far, but she is willing to concede that she handled it badly," Vivien said as she took a seat near the hearth and began to remove her gloves. "Father had a lot to do with it, I'm sure. When he heard what had happened, he and Mother spent a good deal of time speaking together in her sitting room."

Kingsley took a seat across from his sister. "How do you know all this?"

"Haven't you learned by now, I'm very observant. Besides, you can thank me for being the one who mentioned today's events to Father. I felt it only fair he be kept informed that my siblings and I had lost our favorite governess. I was so distraught to think there'd be no more Italian lessons." Her fluttering lashes and coy grin led Kingsley to believe his younger sister had managed to work her feminine magic on their father.

He smiled at the resourcefulness of his little sister. "Aren't you the busy one?"

"I've had little else to keep me busy. It's been dreadfully boring at the cottage this summer. Not at all like it used to be when we were all here together. And since Thomas left last week to travel to Newport with that dreadful Harry Lehr, I've had nothing other than your affair with Anna Maria to keep me occupied. There's nothing wrong with interfering when my favorite brother's happiness is at stake."

147

Since Vivien had openly acknowledged her intention of becoming Mrs. Thomas Hollingsworth, it seemed only reasonable his departure from Tarrytown had left his sister searching for more stimulating diversions. Nonetheless, it was somewhat off-putting to know his personal affairs had become her personal pet project.

"Where do you think she's gone? I went to the train station, but it was already closed for the night." Kingsley informed her.

"I know. I had Mr. Miller stop at the station," she said, referring to their head groomsman. "Turns out, he knows the station clerk. We hunted him down and he confirmed that a man and two women took the last train to New York. From the description I provided, the clerk was fairly certain the two women were Mrs. Dorvall and Anna Maria. At least we know she's not alone and she's headed for New York. It's a start."

Kingsley sat back, impressed. "You really are quite the detective, aren't you?"

Vivien ran a hand over her lap to smooth out her skirt. "I suggest we contact Mrs. Dorvall as soon as we reach New York. It's very likely she'll know where Anna Maria has gone."

"We?" Kingsley asked, with a lift of his brow.

"Certainly. You don't expect me to let you go running off on this little adventure without me. I've also taken a room here. My maid is there now with my bags. I had a dreadful time trying to convince Mother to let me come, but after I spoke to Father, it was so much easier. Father understands how vital our support is, even if Mother is still resistant."

"You said she feels dreadful."

"She feels dreadful that she upset you, and that you've gone running after our governess. I doubt she's disappointed that Anna Maria has left. She's hoping this is nothing more than a momentary fling, but I have a feeling Father is on your side."

"I can assure you, this is more than an affair. I've asked Anna Maria to marry me."

"Kingsley, that's wonderful. All the more reason you need my help. It will look much more respectable to search for her with me by your side. And when you find her, which I'm sure you will, I'll be there to ensure you don't say the wrong thing."

"I hardly think I need my little sister advising me on how to run my love life."

"Oh, really. That isn't what you said a week ago."

"That was before I was certain Anna cares for me. And I know she does." *Or at least she did.* Admittedly, he might not know much about women—most men didn't—but he did know they didn't share passionate kisses with men they didn't like. Especially not a woman as proper as Anna Maria Lucci. "It's Mother's meddling that has her taking off like this. I had planned to announce our engagement this Sunday at dinner with everyone present. Now, instead, the house will be a buzz with rumors and there'll be no announcement to celebrate."

"I agree, it's unlikely you're going to get the big family celebration you had hoped for, but that doesn't mean there can't be an announcement. I suggest placing one in the New York *Times* when you're ready to announce to the world that you're to be married."

For a brief moment, he thought his sister had gone mad, but just as quickly he saw the benefit of her plan. Once he announced his engagement in the *Times*—if Anna Maria would still have him—his mother would have no other option than to support his marriage. If not, she risked making their family the subject of society's punitive rumor mill, and Kingsley was fairly certain that was the last thing Edith Goddard wanted.

Now all he had to do was find Anna Maria and pray to heaven she still wanted to become his wife. Perhaps this was where a bended knee would come in handy.

~*~

Grateful for his company, Anna Maria sat with Mr. Vanderzeit in the luxurious restaurant of the Park View Hotel sipping her tea as she tried to relax while she took in her surroundings. Dark wood paneling trimmed the hunter green walls and massive crystal chandeliers hung from the ceiling. Café style tables scattered throughout the room were

149

inlaid with exotic woods and mother of pearl, and the accompanying chairs were pleasantly overstuffed, inviting a guest to sit and stay a while.

Mrs. Dorvall had been with them earlier when they arrived, but had stepped away to speak with her husband, Richard Dorvall, the owner of the hotel. Though Bernice Dorval walked with grace and dignity, Anna had noticed her slight limp and was reminded of the stories she had heard in the servant's hall. Apparently, when she was still a young debutante, Bernice Beaumont had suffered a significant injury in a carriage accident—it was rumored to have been a broken hip—and for years she had stayed away from society, remaining at home with her mother. Her father's death in the accident had left her mother mourning. It was only a few years ago that Bernice had made a return to society, and in a very short time, had managed to marry Richard Dorvall, one of the wealthiest men in New York. From Anna's limited observation, they seemed a very happy couple. Theirs was a relationship to be admired.

Earlier, when they had all arrived at the Park View Hotel, Mrs. Dorvall had insisted on putting Anna in one of their finer guest rooms, and had told her she could stay as long as she needed. While such generosity was beyond belief, Anna had every intention of limiting her stay, and expressed her intention to book her passage to Italy on the first available ship. The thought of leaving New York felt like a death blow— she had come so far with such great expectations—but the humiliation Mrs. Goddard had inflicted upon her cut like a knife to her heart.

Signore Kingsley had led her astray down a rosy garden path as he seduced her, and all the while, he had encouraged her to believe she could be his wife. He must have known his family would never approve of such a union. For such deceit, she had no forgiveness. Worst of all was the embarrassment of knowing she had allowed herself to believe a man of Signore Kingsley's standing had wanted to marry a lowly governess, even though she knew better.

When she had enquired at the front desk about ships sailing for Italy, she had been told there was one leaving in two days for Genoa. It wasn't exactly Rome, but at least she could take a train from there to her home in Ferentino. Sadly, she had also been informed that unless she wanted to travel in steerage, the cost of booking passage back to Italy was more than she could afford. The idea of traveling alone in a section designated for single men and the desperately poor seemed not only improper, but somewhat dangerous. Which meant she needed to earn additional money if she wanted to travel in second class when she returned home.

"It looks as though I'll be staying here in New York longer than I had hoped," she commented to Mr. Vanderzeit. "The cost of a second-class ticket is more than I can currently afford. I'll need to do something to add to my savings."

Mr. Vanderzeit eyed her with a look of honest concern. "If you're certain you want to return to Italy, I will gladly pay your passage, although I suggest you may want to wait for a ship traveling directly to Rome. It will save you the long train ride. And I insist on first class. It's only fitting considering I'm the one who encouraged you to come to New York."

For a brief moment, Anna Maria considered accepting his generous proposal, but firmly decided against it. Her sense of independence would not allow it. "I appreciate your offer, Mr. Vanderzeit, but it's time I looked out for myself. I'll either travel in third class steerage, or I'll find a way to earn what I need."

"As you wish, Miss Lucci, but please know I only have your best interests at heart."

Even if she could afford the transatlantic ticket, she was somewhat reluctant to return to her father's house. To do so would only be an admission of failure, and she hated to think she had come so far only to go back to where she had started.

What she needed was to find another position as a governess for another wealthy family, but without proper references from her last employer, it was unlikely anyone of any financial standing would be willing to employ her. Since she had no reason to believe Mrs. Goddard had anything nice to say about her, it was highly doubtful the woman would give her a proper reference.

However, she still had a letter of recommendation from Mrs. Dover. Maybe she could look for work in one of the state-run orphanages, or if she were truly lucky, a respectable private school for girls would be willing to take her on. Wouldn't that be grand?

Bringing her attention back to the moment, Anna looked up from staring glassy-eyed at her teacup straight into the steady gaze of Mr. Vanderzeit. It was somewhat disconcerting to know he had been watching her.

After taking a drink of tea, he asked, "So tell me, Miss Lucci, are you enjoying your stay in New York?"

Anna set down her cup and forced a smile for the man who had done so much for her. "It seems strange not to be working. I can't thank Mrs. Dorvall and her husband enough for their generous hospitality, but I wish there was some way I could repay them." Since they didn't have children, she couldn't offer her services as a governess. She had let them know, if they had any guests from Italy, she would be happy to assist as a translator, but currently there were none at the hotel. If it were at all possible, she hoped to avoid becoming a chambermaid, but would do anything required to earn her keep and secure her passage back home.

"This is a rather large hotel, there are plenty of empty rooms. Trust me, you are no burden here at all," Mr. Vanderzeit assured her.

"That's what Mrs. Dorvall said, but still, I'm not used to this much free time. I prefer to feel useful." If she were back with the Goddards or even the Dovers, she would be giving lessons to her students instead of relaxing with a cup of tea and chatting with Mr. Vanderzeit, not that she didn't enjoy his company. He was all that was charming and kind, even if he often said things that befuddled her more than a little.

"Have you ever noticed how very little time you spend appreciating the present?" Mr. Vanderzeit asked unexpectedly, as if to prove her point.

"I suppose I've never really thought about it." She'd probably been too busy doing something productive to have time for such thoughts.

"Most people spend their time worrying about the future instead of enjoying the present moment. Or they base their present on their past, and then try to figure out their future based on what they've experienced before, in the past."

Anna blinked as she tried to keep pace with Mr. Vanderzeit's comments, but wasn't sure she had succeeded. "I appreciate every day of my life."

"Do you really? Oh, I'm sure there are moments of each day that you appreciate, such as when you stop to smell the roses, or sit to enjoy a cup of hot tea with a friend." He lifted his cup to take a sip. "But even then, I would wager, much of your mind is thinking about your past. Thinking about what has already happened, or perhaps worrying about your future, thinking about things that may never happen."

"I suppose that's true, but surely it's only natural to wonder what the future will bring. And how else can we evaluate any given situation, if not by our past?" Especially when her own future seemed so unsure at the moment.

"Might it not be possible to benefit from believing that each moment is unique, presenting us with unique opportunities to make choices we might never have considered before?" Mr. Vanderzeit asked.

Suddenly, Anna Maria had the strongest urge to pour out her heart and soul to this man. For months, she had yearned for someone to confide in, someone to tell her troubles to, but it had felt as if she had no one she could trust, no one close enough to hear her story and listen without judgment. Even though Miss Vivien had offered to be her friend, Anna hadn't felt comfortable sharing such private thoughts with her young student. And while it could be said that she hardly knew Mr. Vanderzeit, in her heart she felt she could trust him. Surely, he would understand her concerns in ways no one else could.

"Oh, Mr. Vanderzeit, if only I knew what to do. When you first gave me the opportunity to come to America, I believed it was an answer to my prayers, an opportunity to move away from my father's strict temper, and live independently on my own. But what I didn't consider is how alone I would be. Prior to this, I've always been surrounded by family and friends. Dear friends who love me. But here, I feel alone. I'm not one of the downstairs servants, and as such, I'm not warmly welcomed into their circle. But I'm certainly not on equal footing with the families I serve. To them, I'm only one of their servants, employed to do as they order, and if they don't like me, they have the power to send me away at a moment's notice. Which they do. First Mrs. Dover, and then Mrs. Goddard. She thinks me a liar, and a shameless gold digger after her son's money. Oh, I know, she may not have said it outright, but we both know what she meant. I'm not good enough to sit at her table, much less marry her son. I knew she would never approve. What was Signore Kingsley thinking? Society will never accept a poor Italian governess as his wife."

"Do you really believe Mr. Goddard was thinking about his social standing when he asked you to marry him?"

"No, of course not. But his mother thinks of such things, and she will never approve." Edith Goddard had made that abundantly clear.

"Kingsley Goddard is a grown man. If he's truly a man of his word, as you believe, I'm sure he'll set things right. If not, well then, my dear, aren't you better off without him?"

Anna stared wide-eyed at Mr. Vanderzeit. What he said was perfectly true, but to hear it stated so blatantly caused her heart to throb painfully in her chest.

He reached out and patted her hand. "Aren't you getting ahead of yourself? Isn't it much better to simply enjoy this moment? You're sitting in a beautiful hotel, enjoying a splendid cup of tea, and I would hope you find my company enjoyable."

"Oh, yes, Mr. Vanderzeit, you're most charming and kind. I couldn't ask for better company. It's just that I feel . . ."

"Adrift?"

"Yes, that's right, adrift. I feel adrift in a sea of the unknown."

"Might it not more rightly be considered a sea of possibilities. Think about it, my dear. At the moment, you have no cares, no woes. Only grand possibilities of what the future may hold. Rather than fussing yourself with worries about all that can go wrong, would it not be so much better to contemplate all that could go right?"

"Other than taking advantage of Mr. and Mrs. Dorvall's kind generosity, which I can assure you, I have no intention of doing, what could possibly go right?"

"You're safely lodged in a respectable hotel, having tea with someone who only has your best interests at heart. For the moment, what more could you need? I suggest you sit back, relax, and let the future unfold. It really is the only way to truly appreciate the journey." With that, Mr. Vanderzeit sat back, picked up his teacup, and took a sip. "Ah, it's gone cold. Should we call for a fresh pot?"

Could he really be serious? Her life was on the brink of disaster, and his only concern was calling for a hot pot of tea. If only she could be so carefree. Looking down at her empty teacup, it occurred to her that she really had nothing better to do. Perhaps she should follow Mr. Vanderzeit's suggestion to simply enjoy the moment. With a shrug of her shoulders, she said, "Yes, I suppose I can do with a bit more tea."

CHAPTER 15

The moment they arrived in New York, Kingsley hired a cab to take them to the Park View Hotel.

"Mrs. Dorvall's husband owns the hotel. I'd bet money Bernice took her there," Vivien informed him.

Kingsley gave his sister a dubious look. An understanding of Anna Maria's financial situation was apparently not her strongest asset. "Anna Maria can hardly afford to stay at the Park View."

"I'm sure Bernice will offer her assistance. Why else would she have taken Anna Maria back to New York?"

"All we know for certain is that Mrs. Dorvall gave her a ride to the train station in Tarrytown."

"And that she accompanied Anna Maria on the train. It only makes sense that Bernice offered her a room at the Park View."

"But Anna cannot afford to stay there," Kingsley repeated. Was his sister not listening to anything he said?

"Really, Kingsley, do you think Bernice would charge her? More likely, she believes she's rescuing Miss Lucci from the clutches of our mother."

"A bit overly dramatic, don't you think?"

"More like romantic, and from what I know of Bernice, I'd wager she's a big supporter of romance. Don't you recall how she met her husband?"

"Hardly. I prefer not to bother with such gossip." Although from the look in his sister's eyes, he had the feeling he was about to be subjected to just such an activity as they made their way through the streets of New York.

"Bernice had just made her debut when she was in a terrible carriage accident. I think she must have been only eighteen or nineteen. Her father died in the accident and her mother was badly injured. Bernice suffered a broken hip and I heard it took months for her to heal. Surely, you've noticed that she walks with a limp, although it's much less noticeable these days than it once was. Anyway, after the accident, she stayed with her mother in New Haven while they both convalesced. For several years, they simply dropped out of society. Then, a few years ago, the Delafields held an anniversary ball for their daughter Caroline and her husband, Matthew Beaumont. Bernice is Matthew's sister and he must have convinced her to attend the ball. Surely, you remember the Beaumonts' anniversary ball."

"Can't say that I do." To Kingsley, all balls were the same. Forgettable.

"Not surprising, I suppose. It was a few years ago. Anyway, that's where Bernice met Richard Dorvall, and apparently, it was love at first sight. They were married within the year."

Love at first sight! Is that what had happened to him and Anna Maria? He certainly had taken notice of her that first day when he met her in the upstairs classroom, and while her appearance would incite yearning in any warm-blooded man, he wouldn't exactly say he had fallen in love. Extreme attraction, maybe, but love, that had taken some time.

As he thought back over his time with Anna Maria, it seemed the foundation had been there right from the start, and as they progressed through their sessions together they had built upon that foundation. Rather quickly, the framework of their relationship had taken shape, and with proper attention to detail, it was likely to stand the test of time. At least their relationship *had* been progressing nicely. That was before his mother took it upon herself to tear off the roof with her needless meddling. Who knew what damage she might have inflicted on his bourgeoning romance with Anna Maria. If his mother's harsh treatment of Anna Maria caused her to end their relationship, he might never forgive her. He certainly wouldn't be visiting her at Riverwood anytime soon, or even in New York for that matter. If Anna Maria wasn't welcomed at her table, he had no desire to be there either.

It was best not to think about that now. For the moment, all he could think about was finding Anna Maria and trying to mend the damage his mother had done.

Roused from his tangled web of thoughts, Kingsley heard his sister say, "Mother and Father of course went, but I was too young. I'm sure she made a beautiful bride."

"Who made a beautiful bride?"

"Why, Bernice, of course. Haven't you been listening?"

"Of course, I've been listening. Mrs. Dorvall met her husband at a Delafield ball, they got married, and she made a beautiful bride." There may have been a part there in the middle that he missed, but surely he had gotten the gist of it all.

Finally, after what seemed like hours but was probably no more than thirty minutes, the hired cab pulled up to the Park View Hotel. The moment it stopped rolling Kingsley opened the door and stepped down to the curb. He was about to race through the front doors when he remembered his manners and turned to assist his sister from the cab. Another second or two wouldn't make a difference, he supposed, but he did wish she would hurry.

Once inside the stately hotel, he went directly to the front desk. "Can you tell me if there is a Miss Anna Maria Lucci registered here?" he asked, though he doubted his sweet Italian governess would indulge in such extravagance.

Vivien, only steps behind, came to stand at his side as the desk clerk thumbed through the hotel's register.

"I'm sorry, sir, I don't show a Miss Lucci staying in one of our rooms," the clerk replied after completing his search of the records.

"That's impossible," Vivien said, sounding surprisingly irritated.

"I told you she wouldn't be here," Kingsley huffed, wishing for once he hadn't been right. Not that he was willing to give up. Hopefully, if they could find Mrs. Dorvall, she'd be able to provide some information on Anna's whereabouts.

"I can't believe Bernice didn't bring her here," Vivien murmured incredulously. "That doesn't make any sense." Smiling prettily at the clerk, she added, "Please check again."

"Do you know when she was expected to check in?" the clerk asked, looking somewhat insulted at having his competency questioned. It appeared Vivien's attempt at charm wasn't working on this man.

"Last night. She was traveling with Mrs. Dorvall. Her husband owns this hotel," Vivien supplied briskly before Kingsley had a chance to speak. It seemed his sister was taking it upon herself to conduct this inquiry.

"I am perfectly acquainted with Mrs. Dorvall," the clerk said stiffly. "I wasn't on duty at the time, but I understand Mrs. Dorvall did bring a guest to the hotel last evening. However, if she isn't listed in the guest's registry, it's quite possible she doesn't wish to be found."

"I doubt that's the case," Vivien countered.

"I can assure you, we respect the privacy of our guests," the clerk shot back.

Putting a restraining hand on his sister's arm, Kingsley said, "Perhaps it would be better if we simply spoke to Mr. and Mrs. Dorvall. Do you know where we can find them?" While he appreciated Vivien's desire to help, it seemed her emotions were not helping the situation and he needed her to calm down. "We're friends of theirs," he added for good measure.

"I can let Mr. Dorvall know you're here," the clerk replied, sounding a bit more amenable to Kingsley's request. "Whom should I say is calling?"

"Kingsley Goddard, and his sister, Miss Vivien Goddard." He reached into his coat pocket and pulled out a calling card to hand to the clerk.

"Very well. If you'll wait in the lobby, I'll see if he's available."

159

Kingsley stepped away from the registration desk, but found it impossible to sit down. Instead, he began pacing back and forth. Vivien had no such problem, and took a seat on one of the overstuffed sofas decorating the spacious lobby.

"I knew she wouldn't be here," Kingsley hissed as he passed in front of her. "We're wasting our time." Pressure was building behind his temples and the need to let off steam overrode his usual restraint.

"I still believe Bernice will know where she is," Vivien stated calmly. "We're not wasting time, we're following her trail."

Kingsley darted a stunned glance at his sister. When had she become such a little detective?

Several minutes later, a man smartly dressed in a business suit approached them and introduced himself as Richard Dorvall. Stocky and well built, he appeared as though he were fairly confident he could solve any problem he might encounter concerning his hotel. "How may I be of service?" he asked.

"I'm Kingsley Goddard, and this is my sister, Miss Vivien Goddard. Our mother is friends with your wife, Bernice. I understand she traveled from Tarrytown yesterday with a woman from our household, Miss Anna Maria Lucci. She's been a governess for my sister, and we were wondering if you, or your wife, might know where she's staying while she's in New York."

"Goddard? You're George's son, aren't you?"

Kingsley nodded. "That's correct, now about Miss Lucci—"

"I know your father well. Helped me with some financing for the new kitchen equipment I required. Is there any problem concerning Miss Lucci?" Mr. Dorvall asked.

"No, not at all, I can assure you. She simply left unexpectedly and we were hoping we could speak with her. We're concerned that she has a proper place to stay while she's, umm, visiting New York. If needed, we have a home here in the city where she's welcome to stay." Although he hadn't discussed such an arrangement with his father, according to Vivien, he had Father's support. And since he still had every intention of marrying Anna Maria, he hoped she would agree to stay with Vivien at

160

the Goddard family home until other arrangements could be made. Especially since Mother was still out at Riverwood.

"My wife has given her a room here at my hotel, but if you think she would be happier staying with you, I can certainly pass along your kind offer."

"Is she here now? May we see her?" Kingsley asked, feeling a spark of hope.

"I'll have to ask her. If you don't mind waiting a while longer, I'll see if she's available." It was obvious Mr. Dorvall took the care of his guests quite seriously.

Kingsley breathed a sigh of relief. "That would be wonderful. We'll wait right here."

Mr. Dorvall headed off toward the hotel's elevators while Kingsley continued to pace the hotel lobby. What if he lost her? The thought had banged around in his head since he had learned of his mother's disastrous actions. What if his mother had broken the foundation of trust he'd been building with Miss Lucci? And what if he couldn't fix it because he didn't have the right tools, the right words to put it back together again?

A long night of self-reflection had given him time to realize his mother wasn't the only one to blame, although she had done more than her fair share of damage. He was also to blame for the way he had handled his attraction to Anna Maria. Right from the start, he should have let her know he was willing to choose her over his family, but he hadn't. Not really. Repeatedly, he had told his family he was only interested in her as a tutor, someone to help him with the Italian translation he needed. Even when Jayson pointed out his obvious attraction, he had denied it, claiming he was only looking out for her best interests as a governess in his mother's household. Because that was safer than revealing how much he liked her, how much he *wanted* to spend time with her. He had told Anna Maria it didn't matter that she was a governess working for his mother, even tried to convince himself that was true. It wasn't until he'd been forced to honestly profess his feelings for her that he had finally stood up for her.

161

He thought taking her to Tarrytown, and insisting she use the front door of his home, had demonstrated his support of her, but even then, he had done his best to hide the truth from his mother, telling her it was another tutoring session instead of being honest about his desire to court a governess.

He had told himself it was only because he was being cautious, and considerate of Anna Maria's feelings, not wanting to push too hard, too fast, or too soon. After the wretched embarrassment of his failed first kiss in the library, he had told himself he needed to tread lightly with Anna Maria, but in truth, it was his fear of rejection and the possibility of harsh judgment from his family that had caused him to proceed in relative secrecy.

And now, because he had hidden his true feelings for her, she had been unjustly accused of shamefully seeking his attentions, when all along, it was he who had shamelessly pursued her.

~*~

After eating breakfast in the hotel's restaurant, Anna Maria returned to her room thinking she would change into something a bit nicer before she went out for a walk. Earlier, when she had entered the public dining room dressed in a grey cotton skirt and white blouse, she had realized quite quickly her clothing marked her as one of the working class. The other men and women staying in the hotel wore expensive fashions that indicated the status of their wealth. While she had neither the means nor the inclination to match such style, the least she could do was dress in a manner befitting the fancy hotel.

When she had retired to her assigned room the night before, she had deemed it the prettiest place she had ever slept in. It was also one of the loneliest. Though the apartment was large and spacious with its own adjoining bath—such a luxury—she felt more isolated than she had in the cell-like room she had occupied at the Goddard summer mansion. Though she was extremely grateful for the generosity of Mr. and Mrs. Dorvall to provide her such a lovely place to stay, all the hospitality in the world couldn't hide the fact that she was all alone in a posh building full of strangers.

Beautiful as it was, Anna was too restless to simply hide away in her room and decided she would take a stroll through the park across the street from the hotel. Wanting to look her best, she changed into her russet silk dress with the matching felted hat Miss Vivien had brought for her in Tarrytown. While no one would be fooled by her outfit into thinking she was one of New York's social elite, at least she would feel less out of place.

She had just taken one last assessing glance in the mirror and was about to step out into the hallway when someone knocked on her door. The unexpected sound startled her and she took a step back. Considering how few people she knew in New York, she cautiously opened the door and was relieved to see Mr. Dorvall standing on the other side.

"Miss Lucci, you have guests in the lobby," he informed her. "Mr. Kingsley Goddard and his sister, Miss Vivien Goddard, have asked to see you."

"Oh, my goodness! Mr. Kingsley is here? To see me?"

"Yes, he is. I believe they've come to offer you a place to stay. I want to assure you, as a guest of my wife, you're welcome to stay here as long as you wish."

While she had no desire to take advantage of Mr. and Mrs. Dorvall's hospitality, she found it hard to believe Mr. Kingsley and Miss Vivien were here to offer her free lodging. "You say they're in the lobby?"

"Yes, Miss. Do you not wish to see them?"

"No, it's not that. It's just that . . . Well, do you have someplace private where we could meet?" She'd already have enough public displays of humiliation. She certainly wasn't interested in setting herself up for another.

"I understand perfectly. If you'd like, I can offer my private conference room. It's right next to my office. I can assure you, no one will bother you there."

Anna didn't know how much Mrs. Dorvall had told her husband about her situation, but apparently it was enough for him to make this kind offer. She was also undeniably pleased to know she was dressed in her finest apparel, since she had no desire to appear before Signore

Kingsley dressed as a governess. Though she was interested to hear what he had to say, she was done taking orders from the Goddard family.

~*~

Too nervous to sit, Anna went to stand in front of the large window of the conference room that overlooked the hotel's courtyard. Mr. Dorvall had left her there while he went to fetch Mr. Goddard and his sister. It was flattering to think Kingsley had followed her to New York, but Anna also felt suspicious. Surely, he knew his mother had declared their engagement unacceptable and had basically sent her packing. What possible motive could he have for tracking her down? Did he actually plan to defy his family's wishes? Such an idea seemed too unlikely for Anna to honestly consider, and while a part of her couldn't help but hope, the more practical, realistic side of her knew it was only her hopelessly romantic heart yearning for something that could never be.

More likely, he simply wanted to persuade her to continue as his Italian tutor and translator. Especially considering he was accompanied by Miss Vivien. No doubt, she would ask Anna to continue as her governess. But those days were over. How could she possibly be in the same house as Kingsley, much less the same room, and not feel the disgrace of having been turned away by his mother?

When the door opened, Anna was relieved to see Kingsley had come alone. Thankfully, whatever he had to say would be done in private. It also led her to wonder if she may have been mistaken about his motives.

Kingsley rushed to her side and without hesitation, pulled her into his arms. "Oh, my God, Anna, thank God you're all right. You don't know how worried I've been."

Anna stood stiffly in his arms until he released her. "Worried? Why should you be worried for my sake? I'm perfectly capable of taking care of myself." Granted, it was helpful that Mr. Vanderzeit had provided transportation to New York and Mrs. Dorvall provided her a place to stay, but even without them, she believed she would have managed on her own.

"I heard what Mother did and I can't tell you how sorry I am. She has no right to meddle in my affairs. Especially not my love life. I'm hoping with all my heart you still want to marry me."

"Marry you? After how your mother treated me, do you really think we can be married?" Perhaps it wasn't right to vent her anger on Kingsley, but by God, she'd had enough of rich people thinking they could tell her what to do. She doubted Mrs. Goddard would ever accept her as a daughter-in-law, and she wasn't so sure she liked the idea of being related to her, either. "Mrs. Goddard made it perfectly clear how strongly she disapproves of me. And she's not the only one. Society will disapprove. Surely, you don't wish to bring that upon yourself."

"I care not one whit what society thinks. What's more important is what you think. I was led to believe you love me."

God, yes, she loved him. But love alone could not change what society would think. "I fear I am not as strong as you."

He reached for her hands and brought them to his lips. "How can you say that? You left your home, your family, your country to travel with strangers to a new country and care for other people's children. With you, they *enjoy* learning Italian. How in the world does that make you weak? You're one of the strongest women I know."

It would be nice to believe that was true, but Anna Maria hadn't seen herself that way. She had always thought she was simply making *safe* choices, but now, hearing it like this from Kingsley, she felt a bit stronger, and stood a bit straighter. With a nod, she acknowledged his compliment.

"Anna, I started to fall in love with you the moment I met you. Every moment we spend together only strengthens my conviction that we belong together. You can't deny, we work well together."

"Yes, as your translator, even as a governess to your brother and sisters, but not as your wife. And I won't return to your home as a governess."

"I want you as my wife, not my tutor. We belong together, like nuts and bolts, like wrenches and pipes. Together we just fit. Without you, I'm useless."

165

Though she was moved by his words, she still had her doubts. "Don't be silly. You'll never be useless. You're an amazingly intelligent man with a great future ahead of you. You can have any woman you want."

The fear that had gripped his face magically transformed into a beaming smile. "Then you must agree to be my wife, because I only want you."

He must be kidding. "Are you sure that's what you want?"

"Never more so."

"But what about your mother? What about society? Do you really want to risk their disapproval?"

"Do you really think I care? You, of all people, should know me better than that. Society can hang itself for all I care. All I want is you. For you to be my wife. Not my tutor, or translator, or my siblings' governess. If you want, we can go away to Italy and never come back. I don't care about New York, I care about you. I'm asking you again, please be my wife. I'll not leave here until you say yes."

A smile spread across her lips. How could she say no after such a heartfelt declaration? "Yes, my dear Signore Kingsley. Yes, I'll be your wife."

He pulled her back into his arms, and this time, she returned his embrace, wrapping her arms around his waist.

Lowering his head, he whispered into her ear. "You won't be sorry. I swear to God, you'll never be sorry. We belong together, Anna Maria. Look how well we fit."

She laid her head upon his shoulder, and a sense of inner peace washed over her, clearing away any lingering doubts she might have held. His was the brawny shoulder of a man who actually worked for a living, and not one who merely sat behind a desk and counted other people's money. The memory of his words brought a smile to her lips. Yes, they fit together very well, and she had no doubt, they would for the rest of their lives.

CHAPTER 16

The next few days went by in a rush of activity as Anna began planning her wedding with the help of Miss Vivien and Mrs. Dorvall. Overwhelmed by all the detail that went into planning a proper wedding, Anna was certain she couldn't have done a thing without their help, and was truly grateful for their assistance and support. Especially their support.

Mrs. Goddard, however, still had not come to visit or offer her blessing. Anna was beginning to wonder if her future mother-in-law would ever accept her. With or without his mother's blessing, Kingsley had insisted on pushing forward. He wanted no delays since he expected to leave for Italy within the month and wanted Anna to accompany him as his wife.

Anxious to share her good news with the man who had done so much to make this all possible, Anna was delighted to hear Mr. Vanderzeit wanted to see her in the tearoom of the Park View Hotel. He was already there, waiting for her when she rushed in, and stood to greet her with a kiss to her cheek.

"You look well, Miss Lucci. Much happier that the last time I saw you."

"I couldn't be happier," she said, clasping his hands. As they each took their seats, she added, "In some ways, I owe it all to you. If you hadn't arranged for me to come to New York, I never would have met

167

Kingsley Goddard. Have you heard, we're to be married?" She showed him the ring Kingsley had put on her finger earlier that morning.

To think that in only two short weeks she would be Mrs. Kingsley Goddard was both thrilling and frightening. Thrilling to know Kingsley really did love her, and was willing to defy his mother to secure their union. But also frightening to know Edith Goddard would be her future mother-in-law. All she knew about society was from a servant's point of view, but once she became Mrs. Kingsley Goddard, she would need to quickly learn the rules if she wanted to fit in. Kingsley, of course, had assured her that wasn't important. He had accepted a job near Florence, and they would soon be leaving for Italy, where she would feel perfectly at home, and his mother would not be an issue. Such thoughts provided a measure of comfort.

"Married! Imagine that. It seems this story has a happy ending after all." Mr. Vanderzeit's broad smile mirrored her joy.

"Miss Vivien Goddard has kindly offered to be my bride's maid. She's helping me plan everything. I couldn't do it without her and Mrs. Dorvall. Especially Mrs. Dorvall. She's been amazing."

"If Bernice is helping you, I'm sure everything will be perfectly beautiful. She's amazingly talented when it comes to romance and fairy tale endings. You should have nothing to worry about."

There was one little problem Mrs. Dorvall hadn't been able to solve and Anna hoped Mr. Vanderzeit would be the answer to her prayers. "Miss Vivien's sisters will also be in the wedding, the twins are to be my flower girls, but I haven't any family here, and considering all you've done for me, I was hoping you would consent to walking me down the aisle."

"Well, now, I hadn't seen that one coming." Mr. Vanderzeit paused for a moment and sat back in his chair, apparently considering her request. "I should warn you, I don't usually make public appearances. I prefer to keep my work private."

Her face must have shown her deep disappointment, because a second later, he added, "But in your case, I suppose I can make an exception. After all, I am responsible for bringing you and Kingsley together." Tapping his spoon lightly against his cup as he idly stirred his tea, he added, "Without me, none of this would have happened. So, yes, I'll walk you down the aisle."

She was grateful beyond belief that he was willing to stand in for her father, but still, Anna couldn't help but wonder if maybe Mr. Vanderzeit was over stating his role in her relationship with Kingsley. How could he have known she would fall in love with her employer's son? Or that he would follow her to New York?

"I am the Maestro." The way he stated his profession made Anna wonder if he had read her thoughts.

"I've been wondering why you call yourself that?" Vividly, she recalled seeing it printed on his business card.

"I orchestrate time, and events, and all manner of fate."

"I remember you said that when we first met, but I had no idea what you meant. I still don't."

"Do you recall *how* we first met?"

"Very clearly. I was running from my father's house and had nearly been struck by a horse and rider, but you pulled me to safety."

"More precisely, I pulled you from death. Had I not been *there*, you wouldn't be *here*. You'd be somewhere else, to be sure, it just wouldn't be here. Life does go on, regardless of when or where you are. I had to do the same for Kingsley, or he too would be someplace else."

Anna felt a humming vibration move through her, as though she were a harp's string that had just been plucked. "I'm not sure I understand what you mean." He couldn't possibly be referring to life after death. The idea was too incredulous to believe.

"Many lives and many deaths. As many as you choose. But for now, at this moment, you are here." He chuckled softly to himself. "Don't you just love that phrase, *at this moment*? ATM. Wait until you see what they will do with that in the future."

"If you're a Maestro, as you say, don't you need to tap a baton, or wave a magic wand, or something like that?"

"You're thinking of someone who conducts orchestras. I orchestrate *time.* Completely different. I don't use a baton or a magic wand, although at times the latter can be quite helpful, if for nothing else than the effect it creates. No, I use portals. Even the first time you arrived here was through a portal, if one can imagine a woman's womb as such. And upon leaving, you'll pass through another portal. But no, I use the portals located here on earth. Most humans can't see them, have no idea they exist, but as you must know, I am no ordinary human."

"I still don't understand. How could anyone orchestrate time? I'll accept that you saved my life, but all that required was pulling me to safety."

"No, my dear, it required me to momentarily *stop* time, and then change its direction. Had I not, those horse's hoofs would have done irreparable damage, and you would never have come to America. Actually, Kingsley had an experience very similar to yours, although I doubt he's any more aware of his good fortune than you are. But really, Anna Maria, you needn't trouble yourself with such thoughts. You're here now, and that's all that matters."

The rational side of her argued that he was merely being a silly old man, making grandiose statements, but another part of her believed he was telling the truth. "I'm not sure if I believe you, but I know I'm grateful for all that you've done."

"Someday you'll understand," he said as he waved his teaspoon languidly through the air.

Anna watched it go round and round in a strangely mesmerizing pattern, unable to look away. When he suddenly stopped, she shook her head, feeling as if she had briefly dozed off.

"Am I to understand, you're to be married?" Mr. Vanderzeit asked, setting his spoon next to his teacup.

Anna blinked a few times, trying to recall what they had just been discussing. "Oh, yes. My wedding. Miss Vivien Goddard has kindly offered to be my bride's maid. She's helping me plan everything. I couldn't do it without her and Mrs. Dorvall. Especially Mrs. Dorvall. She's been amazing. Miss Vivien's sisters will also be in the wedding, the twins are to be my flower girls, but I haven't any family here, and considering all you've done for me, I was hoping you would consent to walking me down the aisle. Will you do that for me, Mr. Vanderzeit? Will you walk me down the aisle?"

Mr. Vanderzeit beamed her a bright smile. "It will be my pleasure. And if I'm to give you away, I should think you can call me Jules."

Anna breathed a sigh of relief. "Oh, thank you, Jules. If it wasn't for you, I'm almost certain none of this would have been possible."

~*~

At the last possible moment, Kingsley's mother and father stepped into the cathedral dressed to perfection and took their seats near the front of the church. It wasn't until later, at the reception held at the Park View Hotel, that Kingsley finally had a moment to speak alone with his father.

"Congratulations, son, you have my best wishes," his father said, clinking his glass against Kingsley's.

They each took a sip of champagne before Kingsley replied. "Thank you, Father. I'm happy you were able to attend my wedding. I know it was rather unexpected."

"I should say so. Only a few weeks' notice. But I'm not surprised. Once you set your mind upon something, there's no stopping you."

"Like father, like son, I suppose," Kingsley said, noting the gleam of pride in his father's eyes. "How did you get Mother to attend?"

"You could say I was rather insistent. I was prepared to drag her here in her nightgown, if necessary, since she threatened to spend the day in bed feigning a headache. Thankfully, in the end, she saw it my way."

Kingsley chuckled along with his father. "I'm glad I have you on my side."

"Don't worry, your mother will come around. All she wants is your happiness. By the time you return with your bride from Italy, she'll have all of Manhattan welcoming you into their homes."

Kingsley hoped that was true. Not for his sake, but for Anna Maria's. He wanted her to feel welcomed and accepted by his circle of friends. "I understand you know Jules Vanderzeit," he said, referring to the man who had walked Anna Maria down the aisle. Surprisingly, it seemed Jules had left the church before the ceremony was over. When Kingsley turned to look for him as he left the altar, Mr. Vanderzeit was no longer in his seat.

His father seemed uncomfortable with the question. "Why do you ask?"

"When we first met, he asked about you."

"Did he? How did you meet?"

"It was the strangest thing. I was watching a bathtub being hoisted up one of the buildings near Branson's office when the darn thing broke the wench and nearly fell on me. If Vanderzeit hadn't pulled me out of the way, it might have killed me. I shall be forever grateful to him for saving me from such a fatal blow."

"That sounds like Vanderzeit. Always in the right place at the right time. Let me warn you, my son, when one is indebted to Jules Vanderzeit, he has some rather unconventional ways of calling in his favors."

"I plan to work on his project in Italy. I'm sure I'll have plenty of opportunities to return his favor."

"Just be careful in the choices you make. When Vanderzeit is around, life has a way of twisting and turning in ways you'd never imagine." His father's warning seemed rather enigmatic, but it reminded Kingsley of his brother.

"I'm not surprised to see Jayson wasn't in attendance." Kingsley had thought about asking his younger brother to be his best man, but in the end, had called upon Max Branson to stand up with him.

"Seems he has better things to do. Last I heard, he's taken in interest in spiritualists and mediums, and all manner of such quackery. Heaven help the lad if he should start believing in all that nonsense."

"That's Jayson for you. I wouldn't worry too much. Give him a month or two and he'll most likely move on to something else."

"One can only hope. But you, Kinsley, now that you're happily married, I expect you'll be heading off to Italy to work on that new project, and taking your bride with you."

"That's the plan. I know she's excited to return home, and visit her family. We sent them a telegram announcing our marriage. I'm not sure

I look forward to meeting her father. From what Anna Maria tells me, he can be rather difficult."

"Much like your mother. Seems only fair you should each have a challenging in-law." Father smacked him lightheartedly across his shoulder.

"Speaking of my bride," Kingsley said, looking across the room to where she stood. "I must be getting back. Don't want to leave her alone for too long."

"Understood." Father nodded with a wink. "Don't let me keep you."

With a parting nod, Kingsley stepped away to join his bride. Placing his hand at the small of her back, he leaned in and nuzzled her ear. "Ready to retire to our room?" he asked, referring to the suite of rooms he had booked at the hotel.

Arching her neck to receive his kiss, she said, "And leave this party full of people I barely know? I should say so."

He understood her meaning. "It won't always be like this." Hopefully, they would soon develop their own circle of friends where Anna Maria could feel welcomed and fully accepted.

"I'm sure you're right. Soon we'll be in Italy, my part of the world, and *you* can know what it's like to be the outsider."

"Except, I intend to be accompanied by my beautiful, Italian-speaking bride, and I'm sure she'll take good care of me. My future's looking rather bright, wouldn't you agree." He wrapped his arms around her waist and pulled her close. Who cared if they were in a room full of people. As newlyweds, this should be expected.

Chuckling softly, she said, "I couldn't be happier for you."

"Ready for me to take you away from all this?" he asked, with a nod toward the crowd.

Looking up at him with shining eyes, she answered, "Yes, Signore Kingsley, more than ready."

AUTHOR'S NOTES:

First and foremost, let me say this book is completely fictional. However, it is inspired by true stories.

While it is NOT true that Consuelo Vanderbilt ever received a marriage proposal from Kingsley Goddard, since the man is completely fictional, it is true that she received a marriage proposal that her mother, Alva Vanderbilt forced her to refuse. Alva wanted her daughter to marry an English nobleman and eventually forced Consuelo to marry the Duke of Marlborough in 1895. According to Consuelo's memoir, *The Glitter and the Gold*, it was a sad failure.

And although Kingsley Goddard and his family are built from my imagination, there is a story told by Elizabeth Wharton Drexel Lehr in her memoir, *King Lehr and the Gilded Age*, on which my book is based. Apparently, Elizabeth witnessed Edith Gould dismiss her Italian governess, Anna Maria Lucci because Mrs. Gould had learned that her son was interested in the young woman. Signorina Lucci insisted that Mr. Kingdom did in fact love her, but she was sent away. Four days later, Kingdom followed Miss Lucci to New York and succeeded in convincing her to become his wife.

Timeless Romance With a Touch of Magic
To find other books of by Tricia Linden please go to:
htpps://tricia-linden.com

Dreaming In Moonlight
Sometimes we wish upon a star.
Sometimes we dream in moonlight.

What he thought was the blessing of a lifetime becomes an unimaginable curse when Lord Gavin Richard Montague, grand duke of Maninberg, agrees to accept immortality from a powerful wizard in exchange for complete control of his kingdom. Now he can never leave.

Besides being a wizard's great granddaughter, Lady Tara Zanders, is an experienced dream weaver who would rather travel the world than submit to seeking a husband. When she finds herself attracted to the charming spellbound duke, her curiosity is aroused and her wanderlust falters. She quickly realizes Lord Gavin is trapped in his kingdom, but she doesn't know why.

There's a battle brewing just outside Lord Gavin's kingdom that threatens Tara's safety. He wants to protect her. She wants to uncover his secrets. Each feels the pull of their passion, but will their well-guarded secrets destroy any hope they may have of finding mutual happiness and truly lasting love?

Until We Meet Again
– A Jules Vanderzeit Gilded Age novel

Victoria Winters doesn't regret her affair at Woodstock, or that she returned from the past pregnant with a daughter who would never know her father. Her only desires are to be a good mother to her daughter and to live happily ever after. That's not too much to ask.

Unfortunately, she's deeply indebted to the Jules Vanderzeit, a mysterious man known as the Maestro who saved her life in exchange for ten years of service as his time-traveling courier. Victoria has spent the last four years caring for her daughter, but she still has time to pay, and now she's being recalled into service to travel to Manhattan in 1888 to retrieve a lost Stradivarius violin.

Jules has tracked the missing violin to Robert Stevenson, a successful investment banker living the good life in the gilded age of Manhattan. After his wife's untimely death, he seeks to employ a new governess for his young daughter. When Victoria shows up at his front door, it's obvious she's the perfect candidate for the job, even though he suspects there's much more to Miss winters than she's willing to tell.

If Victoria can find the violin within three weeks, she'll earn extra time off her ten-year contract with Jules. If she fails, she risks losing her daughter, and possible her life. Before her assignment is over, she'll be forced to decide what she is willing to lose to have everything she ever wanted.

Until Their Hearts Desire
– A Jules Vanderzeit Gilded Age novel

Tessadori Delafield truly loves living in California with her aunt and uncle. When her mother summons her back to New York, she goes with great reluctance, fearing her parents have called her home to see her married to a man of their choosing. The last thing she wants to be is an idle woman, waiting and hoping for a man to make time for her.

Jacob Beaumont is the type of man who could easily capture Tessa's heart, if only he were around long enough to honestly try.

Unfortunately, Jacob has an annoying way of popping in and out of Tess's life like one of those newfangled revolving doors. When she discovers the elusive Mr. Beaumont is also keeping secrets, it's more than Tessa can accept.

Jacob believes he's found the one woman he can't live without, but as long as he is contractually bound to Jules Vanderzeit, that's exactly what he must do. The man known as the Maestro seems intent on keeping Jacob away from Tessa, but with Jacob's mother's life at stake, and Jules holding all the cards, Jacob has no choice but to play by the Maestro's rules.

There's no place like home, but for Tessa and Jacob, finding home means following their heart's desire.

Until You Love Me
– A Jules Vanderzeit Gilded Age novel

More than a century separate **Becky Sue Dobson** and **Rebecca Wheland Jaffray.** One of them is about to discover how deeply their lives are connected.

Becky Sue Dobson lives a dull, middle-class existence in the 21st century. After the loss of her infant daughter, she's ready to end her life. When her car plunges over a steep hillside, instead of death, she encounters a mysterious man called the Maestro. Suddenly, everything she had thought to be true is turned inside out.

In the 1890's, **Rebecca Wheland Jaffary** is living the pampered life of New York's gilded age elite, but after only four months of marriage, she would rather face the scandal of divorce than continue to live with a man she doesn't love. The only reason James agreed to marry her was to secure a loan from her father. Feeling angry and rejected, she runs off to hide at her family's summer home though it's closed for the winter season.

Facing financial ruin after the market crash in May, 1893, **James Jaffray** turns to one of the most ruthless men in all of New York and agrees to marry his daughter, Rebecca Wheland. Though their marriage was never based on love, when she suddenly disappears, James realizes his wife wants nothing to do with him.

Seven days later, when Rebecca returns home, James suspects something is strangely different, but he's not sure what or why; because prior to her disappearance, James hadn't believed he could ever love his wife.

Tricia Linden, author of timeless romance with a touch of magic.

An International Banker by trade, and a romance writer by desire.

In this lifetime, I've lived in five states, on two islands, and on a farm, and am now living in Northern California. My travels have taken me to Guam, Canada, Mexico, Australia, Hong Kong, England, Scotland, several countries in Europe, and several states in the US. Besides my love of reading and writing romance, I have a great fondness for zydeco dancing, classic rock and best of all, Pink Flamingos. Over the years, I've gathered a rather large collection of the fun pink birds.

I believe as spiritual beings, we've been here before and we'll be here again. I believe what happens along the way is part of a grand and glorious adventure that never ends. I believe there can never be too much romance or too much love in the world.

Website: https://tricia-linden.com/
Facebook: https://www.facebook.com/TriciaLindenAuthor/
Tweeter: @TriciaLinden69
Email: Tricia.Linden@ymail.com

www.ingramcontent.com/pod-product-compliance
Lightning Source LLC
Chambersburg PA
CBHW032010170626
46807CB00006B/2734